Cold  Blood

Cold Blood

LEO BRUCE

ACADEMY
CHICAGO

Copyright © Leo Bruce 1952

This edition published in 2019 by Academy Chicago Publishers
An imprint of Chicago Review Press Incorporated
814 North Franklin Street
Chicago, Illinois 60610
ISBN 978-0-89733-038-1

Library of Congress Cataloging in Publication Data
Croft-Cooke, Rupert, 1903-1980
  Cold blood.
Reprint of the 1976 ed. published by I. Henry
Publications, Hornchurch, Eng.
  I. Title.
PR6005.R673C6   1980   823'.912   80-24027
ISBN 0-89733-039-9
ISBN 0-89733-038-2 (pbk.)

Cover design: Lindsey Cleworth Schauer
Interior design: Nord Compo

Printed in the United States of America

1

The Ducrow Case seemed to change Sergeant Beef. I who had known him for many years and chronicled no less than six of his investigations, found myself astonished again and again by his behaviour during this one. It was not that he lost his somewhat boyish sense of humour, or his taste for beer, or his habit of making portentous announcements, or that he ceased to be, in outward appearance, the heavy English policeman with the ginger moustache moist at the tip from immersion in a pint glass. It certainly was not that he was any less astute in his work, or in a certain way, any less successful.

It was as though for the first time in his life he was in what is rightly called "deadly" earnest. For the first time in his life he was a little bit afraid. For the first time he was consciously nothing less than the protector and avenger of society working against a force which he did not underestimate.

I respected this new Beef. I was with him during most of the long and, as it turned out, dangerous investigation and I was glad to see that though the old chuckle was still heard at times, and the old childish mysteriousness maintained, he had it in him to rise above buffoonery and tackle a very unpleasant reality.

The case opened conventionally enough. We had both read newspaper accounts of a murder in Kent and discussed them casually. For a man in Beef's position, any murder has more than academic interest and I remember pointing this out to him on the morning when the newspapers first gave details of the Ducrow affair.

"You should read that," I said, handing him the paper.

"Why?"

"Because I have made you one of the most famous of private investigators. You never know when you may be called into a case like this."

He gave me a rather curious look.

"You know, Townsend," he said, "you amaze me sometimes. *Made* me a famous investigator! My work has nothing to do with it, I suppose?"

"You find the solution, Beef, but that's not the essential, nowadays. Which investigator doesn't find the solution? You need a great deal more than successful detection to make you famous as a detective. You need a peculiar appearance, for one thing. Either enormously tall or minutely small. Very fat or almost wasting away. Beard, eye-glass or some such identification mark. You must resemble an alligator every few pages, like Mrs. Bradley, or talk like a peer in an Edwardian farce, like Lord Peter Wimsey. Or use bits of exclamatory French, like Poirot. You must be different, in other words."

"Aren't I?" demanded Beef.

"You are when I've done with you. But where would you have been without me to bring out all your little oddities? Still in the Force, probably, investigating chicken thefts in a village somewhere. I've made you what you are."

"And not done badly out of it, at the same time."

"I should have done better if I had had better material to work on. You seem to get such sordid crimes. If only you could be given a case with a large fortune involved, like this one. They say that Cosmo Ducrow was worth half a million."

Beef picked up the newspaper and began in his slow and thorough way to read its account of the case. This was written in words which doubtless were considered by their writer to be snappy and terse, but I shall state the details then known in my own way.

Cosmo Ducrow had inherited a large fortune from his father, a shipbuilder of the Antony Gloster type. Cosmo was a strange neurotic man who shunned everything public and had few contacts with the outside world. Later I was to hear him described as a hermit-crab, a creature so sensitive that it can only live in a cockle shell, and dies if it is touched.

Long ago he had purchased for himself a large Georgian house near a Kentish village called Hawden, about forty-five miles from London. He rarely left its grounds. In his fifties, he had already abandoned most activities which hold other men far longer, not even handling a car for himself but keeping a chauffeur to drive his Daimler on the few occasions on which he ventured beyond his lodge gates. The reason for this isolation was usually thought to be shyness, but I think it went farther than that and was pathological. He hated to meet people and was uncomfortable with any stranger.

Ten years previously he had done what many a rich man of indifferent health has done—he married his nurse. Freda Ducrow was twelve or fifteen years younger than he was, a handsome woman of strong passions and decisive will. The two appeared to be fairly happy together, however, and Freda

Ducrow had grown adept at shielding her husband from unwelcome contacts.

Their home, Hokestones, was large and grey, planted about with huge, rather gloomy trees and out of sight of the road. I found it later a melancholy place, but it was considered to be a fine piece of period architecture, and some of the pictures and furniture were of great value.

At the time of Cosmo's death there were living in the house the man himself and Freda, a lifelong friend of Cosmo's named Theo Gray, a secretary and agent, Major Gulley. This agent, as a matter of fact, was shortly to move into a cottage on the estate, which was vacant and had been furnished for him. As domestic servants there was a man named Gabriel and his wife Molly, who had worked at Hokestones for many years. There was also Mills, the chauffeur, a younger man but still nearer thirty than twenty.

The main gate had a lodge on each side of it, one of which had been enlarged and accommodated Cosmo's nephew Rudolf Ducrow and his wife Zena. In the other lodge lived Dunton the gardener. They were five hundred yards from the house.

On the night of Cosmo's death the Gabriels went to bed at nine-thirty and Mrs. Ducrow, who had been up to London that day, retired soon after ten, leaving her husband alone with Theo Gray since Major Gulley was away for the night. It was a cold night, and the two men enjoyed a whisky and soda by the fire. Then Theo Gray decided that it was time for bed and went upstairs, while Cosmo went along to the library. Gray calculates that this was about eleven o'clock. Cosmo and his wife had separate bedrooms, but Mrs. Ducrow heard Theo Gray pass her door to reach his room.

At four o'clock in the morning Theo Gray, whose room overlooked the drive, was awakened by shouts from the grounds, and looked out of his window. He could see nothing. Some weeks previously two lead figures had been stolen from the garden, and fearing that something of the sort was happening again he telephoned to Dunton the gardener in one of the lodges and told him what he had heard. "You had better keep a look-out," he said.

Dunton pulled on some clothes and hurried out. In a few minutes he saw a man walking from the direction of the house. He concealed himself, intending to surprise and catch the visitor, but when he approached Dunton saw that it was Rudolf Ducrow. He hailed him and Rudolf appeared "very startled and upset" and hurried into his home.

At eight o'clock next morning Dunton found the body of Cosmo Ducrow lying beside a stone seat near the croquet lawn. The back of his head was crushed, and beside him lay the croquet mallet which had, according to expert opinion, been used to give him three or four terrible blows. Rudolf's finger prints were on this weapon.

When Beef had read the newspaper account which embodied most of these facts he thoughtfully sucked his moustache.

"Now, if this was one of the cases that you fellows write about," he said, "it would turn out not to be the nephew at all. But real life's different. How often do you get a string of suspects in real life?"

"I don't know, because by the time we come to read about a case all the suspects not in the running have been eliminated and only the man whom the police believe guilty is being tried."

"Quite right," admitted Beef. "In real life it's usually one of three things. The police haven't a notion and cannot connect anyone special with the crime. Or the murderer is pretty obvious from the first. Or there is not enough evidence. But there aren't many cases when it might be one of a dozen people and the investigator has to decide which is guilty."

"Which of your three do you think the Ducrow case is?"

"Looks pretty obvious, doesn't it? Unless there are things we know nothing about."

It did look pretty obvious, and for the next few days I, in common with most newspaper readers in England, expected to hear of the arrest of Rudolf Ducrow on a charge of murdering his uncle. But the case soon dropped from the front page and no arrest was recorded. I myself began to lose interest and to look elsewhere for a new opening for Beef and me.

It was time Beef tackled another case, and one, I hoped, which would gain for him the sort of recognition which was given to his more aristocratic competitors. How many times in the past had I wished that I had devoted my talents as an investigator's chronicler to someone less crude and homely in appearance, someone with more *savoir faire*, someone of the *haute monde*. I recognized now that it was too late to look for this and that; for good or ill my old friend would continue to be the subject of these memoirs. But as I have explained elsewhere, I myself am of the professional classes—I make no higher claim—a public schoolboy, educated as a matter of fact at St. Lawrence College, Ramsgate, and there are times when it seems that Beef will never rise above the level of a public bar. I therefore hoped that the next case to engage us would at least take us to a higher *milieu*.

The Ducrow case would have done that, I reflected. Rudolf's wife was a daughter of Lord Dunborrow, and Hokestones was quite a famous country house. But if this was not to be, at least I hoped that we should not be engaged on some sordid case which took us to slums and tenements.

One morning Beef rang me up.

"This looks like it," he said cryptically.

"What looks like what?" I asked, restraining my curiosity.

"A case for me."

"For us," I corrected.

"For me, but I daresay you can write it up if this new publisher of yours will take it."

I swallowed.

"If you imagine..." I began angrily.

"Never mind. Listen to this. It's important. I'm being called in on the Ducrow case. Theo Gray is coming to see me today."

"Where?"

"What do you mean 'where'? At my home, of course."

A picture rose to my mind of Beef's little house in Lilac Crescent, one of a dingy row of cottages chosen because they were not far from Baker Street. I remembered the ridiculous brass plate he had set up: "W. Beef, Investigations". I wondered what a man like Theo Gray would make of that.

"Couldn't you have arranged to meet at my flat?" I asked.

"Certainly not. He's coming at four o'clock, so if you're interested you'd better be round before then."

I agreed and hung up. At least, I thought, Beef would have a case.

2

"The trouble is," said Beef while we sat awaiting the appearance of Theo Gray, "you've made me look so silly in some of your books that we can't tell why I'm being called in. This man may be the murderer, for all we know, consulting me because he thinks I shall never find out and he wants to show willing."

"That's an exaggeration," I retorted. "I've always admitted that you've got your man."

"But you've made it look more like luck than judgement very often."

How different, I could not help reflecting, was the conversation of Holmes and Watson while they sat waiting for their clients not half a mile away. If Watson had to make any apology it was for himself, not for the man whose achievements he proudly chronicled, whereas when I looked across the sitting-room at Beef I know how much I had to explain.

There was a short ring at the door and we could hear Beef's wife hurrying forward from the kitchen. I had tried tactfully to explain to her the necessity, on occasions like this, of giving a professional air to the consultation, enquiring the visitor's name and announcing him, but my efforts were in vain. "Gent to see you," she said, pushing her head in and leaving our visitor to come forward after she had returned to the kitchen. We both rose.

Mr. Theo Gray was rather a distinguished-looking man with thick hair prematurely white and a straight soldierly bearing. A clipped moustache and a well-tailored suit emphasized this. He did not look distraught or nervous, but he was clearly not a man to exhibit his emotions.

Beef held out his large red hand.

"This is a pleasure," he said heartily, then introduced me.

Theo Gray wasted little time on civilities.

"I want your help," he said gravely to Beef.

"You shall have it," Beef replied importantly. "I've read what's been published of the case."

"That is very little. There are some baffling features of it which have not been mentioned. What I want you to do is to come down to Hokestones and discover the truth. I should like you to come at once because at any moment the police may arrest an innocent man."

"That's not very likely," cautioned Beef. "The police don't often charge anyone with murder until they're sure."

"But as far as I have been able to gather they *are* sure. They believe that Cosmo Ducrow was murdered by his nephew Rudolf."

"And wasn't he?"

"I beg your pardon?"

"I said, wasn't he?"

"Of course he wasn't. Rudolf was very fond of his uncle and does not know what it means to be covetous. Unless we have that straight it's not much good your working on the case."

I thought it was time for me to interrupt lest Beef by his tactlessness should lose his opportunity.

"What Sergeant Beef intended..." I began, but Beef broke in.

"Look here, Mr. Gray," he said. "You've known this young man for years. You couldn't imagine him doing anything like this. But can you imagine anyone else doing it, for that matter? Murder is always a surprise unless it is just a crime of violence by a thug. Now I'm not saying that I think Rudolf Ducrow murdered his uncle. I don't know anything about it yet. But appearances are very much against him."

"Of course they are. That is exactly why I have come to you. I don't want to see this young man put to the terrible ordeal of a trial. The only way to prevent that is for someone to discover the truth."

"So in your mind discovering the truth and proving Rudolf Ducrow's innocence are the same thing? You're so sure he did not do it that you are employing me to investigate?"

"That is so."

"Why me?" asked Beef suddenly and rather loudly.

There was the hint of a smile on Theo Gray's face as he answered.

"I wanted the best man for the job," he said.

"There's some a lot better known than me," Beef admitted. "Been written up better. Why didn't you go to Poirot, for instance?"

For the first time Theo Gray looked a trifle uncomfortable.

"As a matter of fact, I did make enquiries," he said, "but found that he was engaged on another case."

"What about Albert Campion?"

"Not interested, I gathered."

"So as a last resort you come to old Beef. You know, Mr. Gray, I don't know whether I shan't refuse this case. *Then* where would you be?"

"On the phone to Inspector French..." began Mr. Gray, but Beef was chuckling.

"I'll take it," he said. "Now let's get down to business." To my horror, he pulled out of his pocket one of the old black notebooks which he loved, and licked a stump of pencil. "Tell me what you can about the murdered man."

"Cosmo was a very strange being," began Theo Gray. "He suffered as a boy from being the motherless son of a self-made millionaire to whom he was a great disappointment. His father was, as you know, old Mulford Ducrow, who rose from being a ship's boy to the managing directorship of the Glasgow-Brazilian Steamship Company. He wanted a son to follow him to sea, imagining him a tough, Jack-my-hearty sort of chap, and was bitterly disappointed when Cosmo turned out to be a shy frail youngster more interested in philately than shipping. He bullied and snubbed the boy, and even when Cosmo was in his thirties the old man would shout at him and sneer at him and make him feel more self-conscious than ever."

Beef nodded.

"I know the type," he said.

"I was at school with Cosmo, and at Cambridge. In fact, we spent most of our lives together. I married when I was twenty-seven and my wife died five years later, since when we have remained more or less under the same roof. Cosmo hated and feared new faces, and looked to me to keep him in touch with life, to keep him sane, I sometimes thought.

"When his father died he inherited everything, but it would be difficult to imagine anyone for whom great wealth had so little significance. I persuaded him to buy Hokestones because I felt that he would be happier in a house large enough to give him absolute privacy. He was more easy in mind, more contented, for his first few years there than he ever was, before or since. Then, ten years ago, he married Freda Boyce."

"A very happy marriage, I understand."

"In a way—in a certain way—yes. You will, of course, meet Mrs. Ducrow, and I am not going to say anything which will influence your own impression. What can be said is that Cosmo, from the day of his marriage, ceased to be his own master."

"Had he ever been that?"

Theo Gray looked at Beef as though the question had startled him.

"I see what you mean. You may be right. Never in the sense that most men are. But he did make up his own mind about certain everyday things once, whereas Mrs. Ducrow never even allowed him to choose a suit for himself or decide what time he would dine."

"Yet you say they were happy?"

"In a certain way, I think I said. Cosmo rather liked his life being run for him down to the smallest detail, and so long as he could shut himself up in his library with his unique collection of stamps his family could live as they pleased and spend what money they liked. Cosmo was a gentle man, a recluse if you like, shy to the point of misanthropy, but he was not a fool. If he took no part in managing his own affairs it was because he did not wish to."

"He doesn't sound like a man to have a lot of enemies."

"He hadn't an enemy in the world—at least, so far as I knew. True he kept away from people, but with those whom he did meet and to whom he had become accustomed he was amiable and considerate. The servants, for instance, seemed very fond of him."

"Yet someone did him in..." Beef pointed out crudely.

"I can scarcely believe that it was anyone who knew him."

"A stranger? In that case you've got to suggest a motive. Had he been robbed?"

"No. His wallet and watch were on him. I have told you there are baffling features in this case."

"Tell us about that evening."

"It was such a very ordinary evening, until the tragedy, that there is scarcely anything to tell. Gulley was away. Gulley ran the estate for Cosmo and did any correspondence he needed. Splendid chap. Been with us for years. Cosmo, Freda and I had dinner together. Freda had had a long day in town and went to bed early. Cosmo and I had a last whisky and soda. He was talking about some stamps, I remember. He was going to send Gulley to a stamp auction, as he had done several times in the past. Quite animated, he was.

"I left him at about eleven o'clock. He said he would go through to his library for a while, and I was tired. There was nothing unusual in that—he often spent half the night with his stamps.

"Soon after four o'clock in the morning I heard shouting in the garden..."

"What sort of shouting?"

"Ah, that is the difficulty. Inspector Stute asked me the very same question, and I find it hard to answer because in a sense I only heard it in my sleep. At least, I woke knowing that I had heard it rather than heard it direct. You know how you can be awakened from sleep by something, know exactly what it was and wait in full consciousness for it to be repeated.

That's what I did, but it was not repeated. Yet I knew that I had not dreamed it.

"I crossed to the window and looked out but it was a black night and I could see nothing. I listened for a few minutes more but heard no sound. I then went and telephoned to Dunton and told him to take a look round. We had had thieves not long before, you see. Then I went slowly back to bed. What he saw, and what he found next morning, you can hear for yourself."

"Yes," said Beef. "Does Rudolf Ducrow admit being in the grounds?"

"Yes. He spoke to Dunton, in fact."

"How does he account for his presence there?"

"That is one of our difficulties. He has no satisfactory explanation. He says that he could not sleep and decided to go for a walk."

"On a pitch black November night?"

"That is what he says."

"Did he hear any of the shouting which you heard?"

"No."

"That's odd, isn't it?"

"There was a wind. He might have been to leeward of the noise."

"I must say that as the case stands, and on the information I have been given..." Beef began pompously, but broke off to open the door for his wife who had shouted "Will!" from the passage. She entered with a huge tin tray piled with heavy white tea cups and saucers, a plate of thick bread and butter, and to my horror a dish stacked high with shrimps.

"I thought you might like a cup," she said and laid the dining-table while Theo Gray and I watched with some embarrassment.

"I do like a shrimp or two at tea-time," said Beef expansively. "What about you, Mr. Gray?"

"Excellent. Excellent," said Theo Gray thoughtfully and added something about phosphorus.

"Is that what it is?" grinned Beef. "Still, they're very tasty. Now bring a chair up and we can get started."

"Something else happened that night," said Theo Gray, "something I have not told the police. When I was on my way back to my room after phoning to Dunton I was stopped at her door by Freda Ducrow. She was standing there in a dressing-gown. 'What's the matter?' she asked. I told her that I had heard shouts in the garden and had told Dunton to investigate."

"How did she take that?" asked Beef.

"She seemed relieved. Very relieved," replied Theo Gray slowly.

3

We drove down in my car to Hawden, the village near which was Hokestones. It was a rainy dull afternoon, one of the last in November and not, I reflected, the sort of day on which one wanted to come to a gloomy house and grounds in which a murder had recently been committed.

As we approached the lodge gates Beef consulted the notes in his black book.

"That must be Rudolf's house and this one Dunton's."

The iron gates were shut and I sounded my horn. A big red-faced man emerged from the smaller lodge.

"Well?" he asked, not troubling to disguise a natural surliness.

I was about to explain our mission when Beef leant from the car.

"Just open that gate, will you? I'm Sergeant Beef."

Some further explanation was clearly necessary.

"We are investigating the recent..." I began.

But Beef would not allow me to speak.

"Have you any instructions about me?" he shouted at the man.

"You can go through," said Dunton resentfully, and began slowly to open the gates.

"If that's the speed you generally move at," Beef said to Dunton, "it must have been a nice time before you got out when Mr. Gray phoned you on the night of the murder. Still, we'll come to all that in due course. I shall want you for questioning later." Then turning to me he added rather grandly, "Drive on!"

We started to go up the drive, and the house became visible. I suppose that kind of architecture is very fine for those who like it, but I must say that the flat grey front, the regularly spaced windows, the urns along the coping and the hooded front door seemed to me more grandiose than welcoming. The great dripping trees, cypress and cedar and monkey-puzzle, which stood about like gigantic scarecrows did little to relieve the gloom. It took us several minutes to cover the distance from the gates to the front door, but the drive took a winding course and there was doubtless a quicker way.

"I suppose this is what you'd call a mansion, isn't it?" asked Beef, trying not to sound awed.

"It is one of the finest Georgian houses in this part of the country," I said, then added mischievously: "You will soon grow accustomed to staying in a house of this kind."

"What about you?" asked Beef rudely.

"My great uncle..."

"Oh, cheese it, Townsend. You give me the gripes. Come on, let's go and see what to make of this turn-out. Georgian or not Georgian, they've had a murder here. And a very nasty murder at that."

I decided to let this pass, reflecting that Beef was incapable of any refinement.

The front door was opened by a squat, square-headed man who stared at us fixedly.

"You must be Mr. Gabriel," said Beef. "Glad to know you. Nasty day, isn't it?"

I tried to signal to Beef that one should never gossip with servants at the front door, but could not make him see me. Gabriel, addressed in this way by a caller, seemed to have forgotten his manners, too.

"It's a stinker," he agreed. "All right for ducks."

"Army?" asked Beef.

"Gunners."

"Africa?"

"Germany."

"Keep you long?"

"Four years of it."

"What about the *frauleins*, though?"

"Ah!"

I decided to put a stop to this vulgarity.

"Is Mr. Gray at home?" I asked severely.

"Yes. He's in the library. I'll take you through."

"I'd like a word or two with you later," Beef told Gabriel.

"Cern'ly, sarge. Come on down to our sitting-room when you like. If there's anything I can tell you, you're welcome. The police don't find out everything, you know."

I distinctly saw him wink.

"I'll be down presently for a cup of char."

Gabriel ushered us into the library.

Theo Gray in his own surroundings was both more genial and more imposing than he had been in Beef's stuffy little sitting-room. He made us welcome, showed us chairs and rang for tea.

"That's Gabriel, is it?" asked Beef. "How long's he been working here?"

"Since about 1930, though he had four years' war service in that time."

"Seems all right."

"Gabriel? First-rate. Straight as a die. An excellent servant. The only trouble with Gabriel in this affair is that he is unnecessarily reserved. The police complain, in fact, that he is unco-operative."

"Perhaps he doesn't like policemen. There *are* people who don't," said Beef with heavy sarcasm. "Well, this is the library, is it?"

Gray nodded.

"The last time you saw Mr. Ducrow he was making for this room?"

"Yes."

"Kept his stamps here?"

"Those are his albums and specimen cases."

Beef looked about him.

"You didn't tell me there were french windows in this room. Where do they lead?"

"On to the terrace."

"So Mr. Ducrow could have walked out there?"

"Almost certainly did so, I imagine. He had no overcoat on when he was found, as he would most probably have had if he had gone out by the front door."

"What could have taken him out there?"

"That's what you have to find out, surely?"

"I daresay it is. Were these french windows found locked in the morning, or were they open?"

Gray looked at Beef open-eyed, as though he were suddenly realizing something.

"I don't know," he said. "I never thought to ask. It's important too, isn't it? We'll find out from Gabriel."

He pressed the bell.

"Gabriel, you were the first in this room on the morning after the murder, weren't you?"

"So far as I know, Sir."

"Did you find the french windows locked as usual?"

"The police asked me that. I found them unlocked as usual, Sir. You see, even if I locked them up earlier in the evening, ten to one Mr. Ducrow would step out for a breath of air and forget to lock them. I often found them open."

"I see. So although they were unlocked that day you attached no importance to it?"

"No, Sir."

"You may go. You see, Sergeant? We seem to be baffled at every turn. Good point though."

"It's not of any importance," said Beef loftily.

We were interrupted by the entrance of a bald man with a comedian's red moustache.

"This is Major Gulley," said Gray.

Gulley greeted us too heartily, I thought. He had one of those deep plummy voices such as you hear in the more boring guessing-games and general knowledge tests which the B.B.C. puts out as entertainment. His clothes were of expensive and shapeless tweed and his heavy brown shoes highly polished.

"The great sleuth, eh?" he said to Beef. "Well, we need you here, I can tell you. We're all pretty angry about this business and we want it cleared up."

"All but one," said Beef.

"One? I see what you mean. Yes."

I had a quick premonition that Beef was coming out with one of his most gross and tactless broadsides, and shuddered to think of its effect in that quiet, civilized room. Sure enough he did.

"Where were you that night?" he asked Gulley with brutal directness.

The Major seemed only slightly put out.

"In town," he said. "Stayed at the flat."

Gray intervened to explain that the late Mr. Ducrow, though he scarcely ever left Hokestones, kept a service flat in Montrevor House, one of the great blocks of luxury flats in Knightsbridge. It was used by any of the household who wished to stay up there.

"Alone?" asked Beef.

"I beg your pardon?"

"I mean, anyone with you to say you were there?"

Gulley managed to laugh.

"I see. No one else spent the night in the flat, if that is what interests you."

"But you can produce a witness?"

"Really, you know, this is rather offensive, isn't it? Are you suggesting that I need an alibi for Cosmo's murder?"

"I don't know whether you'll need it, but it's a handy thing to have. You benefit under the will, I daresay?"

The bounce and satisfaction were going out of Major Gulley's manner, and he was obviously struggling to keep his temper.

"Yes, I do," he said. "And since you appear to be licensed to ask silly questions, I'll tell you that on that evening I took a lady to dinner and she returned to the flat with me. We remained there for an hour or two, after which I drove her home to Kensington. I have no intention of giving you her name or calling her as a witness, but the porter saw me go out with her. Another porter chatted with me when I left the building next morning."

"No need to get shirty, Major. I've got my job to do."

"Then I suggest you get on with it, instead of asking me a lot of dam' fool questions." He turned to Gray. "I told you it was a pity you couldn't get Poirot or Albert Campion. This case needs tact."

I came to Beef's defence.

"Sergeant Beef believes in bluntness," I explained. "But I am sure it's only his unfortunate manner. It doesn't mean that he suspects you, Sir."

"I suspect everyone," said Beef, "until I know different. I shall want a little talk with you tomorrow, Major, if you don't mind. You will be able to tell me a number of things about the late Mr. Ducrow's affairs."

"Very well," said Gulley. "And I think it's time we all had a drink."

"Now you're talking," said Beef vulgarly.

While we were waiting for Gabriel to appear Beef referred to his notebook.

"On the subject of drink," he said. "Who had what? That night, I mean? Anyone in the house what you might call a real boozer?"

I saw Gray and Gulley exchange glances.

"Since you *have* called him in," said Gulley, "there's no point in not beink frank." Gray nodded and Gulley continued. "Mrs. Ducrow is a lady of temperament. On most occasions she is quite abstemious, but there are times when she... er..."

"She has periods of depression," explained Gray. "Very rare, but sufficient to give us all some anxiety."

"Gin?" asked Beef understandingly.

Gray nodded.

"And she was on the bat at the time of the murder?"

"No. That is… we feared that she might be going to have one of her little spells. She was very lively at dinner, laughing rather unnaturally, we thought. And we knew that she is accustomed to keeping liquor in her bedroom."

"I see. Anyone else?"

"Cosmo enjoyed a whisky but never drank to excess," said Gray. "I myself am no teetotaller but I have never been intoxicated in my life. The same may be said of Major Gulley."

"Fair enough," admitted Beef.

Gulley, looking rather uncomfortable, added, "Rudolf is not a drunkard, but there are times when he is a little unwise. His war service, you know…"

"I shall have to see him tomorrow," reflected Beef. "Well, now I know something about everybody and begin to get the set-up, as they say. It's going to be a very tricky case because none of you can imagine any of the others doing it and you're all going to be cross when you're asked about anyone else. But someone did it, that's certain. That skull was smashed right in by someone. I can't see that an outsider could have had any motive—so there you are. You blame me for asking you questions, Major Gulley, but if you're fair you'll see that I've got to treat you all as suspects."

"The women too?"

"Why not? It would not take a very powerful woman to swing a croquet mallet on to the back of a man's head."

"In that case," said Gulley slowly, "there are two more who haven't been mentioned yet."

"And they?" asked Beef.

"They are Mrs. Gabriel and Rudolf's wife."

"I'm not forgetting them," pronounced Beef.

4

Looking back now to the moment when I first saw Freda Ducrow, I try to sort out my emotions and decide what was her immediate impact on me. Oddly enough I think I felt something not unlike fear, as though she were an almighty schoolmistress who had caught me peeping into things that were no business of mine.

She was a big dark florid woman, and although at a distance she might have been thought handsome, even regal, as she came closer one saw that her features were too heavy and sensual-looking. She carried her tall figure well and dressed as though she wished to look dignified rather than merely attractive. She spoke loudly and insistently, like an actress in a small part trying to be noticed. Her manner to both Beef and me was rather patronizing, but not unfriendly.

I watched her as she entered the room and knew instinctively that although she might be innocent of everything connected with her husband's death, she was yet capable of having murdered him. That passionate face could darken to a fury which would know no restraint.

"Mr. Gray tells me that you are a very experienced detective?" she said to Beef when introductions were over.

"I've worked out one or two cases," said Beef modestly.

"Then you won't fail in this one, I'm sure. The police have been wasting time in trying to implicate my husband's nephew Rudolf. You will be able to start ahead of them. We shall all do our best to give you any information you require."

"Thank you. When was the last time you saw your husband?"

Mrs. Ducrow seemed scarcely prepared to be taken so promptly at her word, but soon recovered from surprise.

"When I said goodnight to him and Mr. Gray that evening."

"There was nothing unusual about him, then?"

"Nothing special. My husband was an unusual man, remember."

"He had no worries?"

Mrs. Ducrow smiled.

"He wasn't as unusual as that," she said. "A man with *no* worries today would be unique, surely?"

"What were his worries?"

"His health. His nervousness and inability to meet people. The welfare of his relatives and friends. He would manage to worry himself if one of the staff was in trouble."

"And was one?"

I was aware of a certain tenseness in the room as Mrs. Ducrow turned to Theo Gray.

"Dunton," she said at last. "His wife is a woman of ungovernable temper. Scarcely sane, I think. She used to work in the house, but we had to dismiss her some months ago. She thought Dunton should give up the lodge and leave us, and when he refused to do so she left him and went to live with her married sister in the village. She has continued to slander us in the most malicious way."

"What does she say?"

"Oh, the usual lies. But Dunton was very worried about it. He is a quiet man who doesn't make friends easily, but he is hard-working and honest. My husband thought a lot of him."

"Otherwise Mr. Ducrow had nothing particular on his mind? No money worries?"

"That would have been the last thing to trouble him, wouldn't it, Theo? He left all his affairs to us to handle."

"Us?"

"Well, to me. But Mr. Gray and Major Gulley advised me. There was nothing connected with money causing any of us worry."

"You're very lucky. Did you hear the shouting in the garden which Mr. Gray heard that night?"

"No. My room faces east. But I heard Mr. Gray pass my door to go downstairs."

"Did he make much noise then?"

"No. But I happened to be awake."

"Do you sleep badly?"

"Not usually. That night I was restless, I think. I waited for his return and asked him what was the matter. He told me and went to bed. I was soon asleep after that."

"And have you absolutely no suggestion to make, Mrs. Ducrow? Nothing that might account for the tragedy?"

"None. I cannot believe that anyone we knew or employed could have done it, and I cannot see why a stranger should have."

It was during the silence which followed that I first became conscious of something which seemed to me in some indefinable way sinister, almost terrifying, in the atmosphere about us. Here was these three people, two men and a woman, sharing something, or oppressed by the same doubts or fears, or, as I thought, in league in some way. They were all watching Beef, who sat there unmoved or unaware, but I had the dark momentary fancy that they were waiting for him to ask some other question, waiting in terror and out of terror ready to strike.

Could Cosmo Ducrow's murder have been planned between them? Was all this rehearsed? Or was it my imagination which filled this quiet room with its high rows of books and thick carpet, this seemingly padded room, with menace? They had all been polite and had answered Beef's embarrassing questions almost without rancour. Was it quite natural for them to be so agreeable?

I am, perhaps, too sensitive to atmosphere but I swear that in that long silence, broken by not even the tick of a clock, I was frightened. I believed that I was in the presence of at least one murderer, who would not scruple to strike again. I am not, I hope, a cowardly man but I almost resolved just then to get Beef aside and persuade him to throw up the case.

He turned over the pages of his notebook, then looked up.

"A nice start," he said. "I shouldn't be surprised but what I might solve this quicker than anyone thinks."

"I hope you do," said Gray quickly.

"There's a few more general questions I'd like to ask while we're all together. First of all, has anyone seen the will?"

"It has been read," said Gray. "Its terms are quite plain. The bulk of the money is left in trust for Mrs. Ducrow, myself and Rudolf, and on the death of any of us who is childless his third of the capital simply remains in the trust for the benefit of the other two. Eventually the money passes to any children we may have or to certain carefully selected charities. But the legacies to employees were unusually large, even for an estate of this size. Major Gulley receives £10,000, the Gabriels and Dunton £3,000 each, while even Mills who has only been with us three or four years gets £2,000."

"Will made some time ago?" asked Beef.

"No. About eighteen months back."

"I see. Now about this croquet. Did anyone play the game?"

Gulley answered this time with a rich, throaty chuckle.

"Indeed we did. All of us. It was the one game Cosmo enjoyed. And very good fun, as a matter of fact."

"What do you play it with?"

"Balls," said Major Gulley. "Wooden balls and mallets. You hit them through hoops. A mallet looks something like a sledge-hammer only it's all wood."

"Did each of you have his own mallet?"

"Not really. We took any one we found. Rudolf had a favourite, though."

"And the one thought to be used in the murder was this favourite one of Rudolf Ducrow's?"

"Yes."

"So there was nothing funny about it having his fingerprints on it?"

Gray coughed.

"I pointed that out to the police," he said, "but I gathered that they still thought it pretty incriminating for Rudolf. You see, if anyone else had used it he would either have left fingerprints himself, or, if he had worn gloves or anything, wiped the others away. Neither of these had happened, it seems."

"Mm. Now the time factor. Does this help at all? You phoned to Dunton within a few minutes of hearing the shouts. He pulled some clothes on and came out in time to see Rudolf approaching his house. Now, presuming the shouts came at

the time of the murder, would the murderer have had time
to reach the lodge gates?"

"Just about, I'm afraid," said Gray.

"Well, I'll go over the ground tomorrow and see what I
think. Now what else is there? Oh, yes, did Mr. Ducrow
have any connection with the Glasgow-Brazilian Steamship
Company?"

"A certain amount of his money remained invested in it,
but he took no part in the direction of its affairs. He was not
even on the Board."

"He had no other relatives?"

"Not that we know of. Rudolf was the only son of Cosmo's
brother who was killed in a car smash about a month after
Rudolf's birth. Cosmo's sister-in-law, Rudolf's mother, died
five years ago. Old Mulford Ducrow was an only son, too,
and Cosmo's mother, who died at his birth, was taken by
the old man straight to church from an orphanage in Malta
in which she had been brought up. So there does not seem
much possibility of unknown relatives."

Beef snapped the elastic of his notebook and beamed on
them.

"Thank you very much," he said. "That's all most helpful.
Now later this evening I want to go and have a chat with the
Gabriels. Will that be all right?"

I was certain now that they watched him uncomfortably. I
was as sure of a threat in the air as one is of a thunderstorm
during the unnatural silence that comes before it.

"Certainly," said Gray at last. "You must question whom you
like. Go where you like. Now I'll show you both your rooms."

Beef was about to say that he had no wish to see his room
till he went to sleep in it, but I managed to signal to him to
go without protest.

When Gray had gone downstairs I went and tapped at Beef's door.

"Hullo," he said. "Going nicely, isn't it?"

"Beef," I said, "let's throw this case up. I don't like it."

"What don't you like?"

"There's something very queer about these people. I had a feeling downstairs that there was some threat hanging over us."

"Funny you should say that. I felt a bit creepy myself. But that doesn't mean any of them's guilty. They've got a lot to hide, that's all."

"You may be right. All the same, I don't like this house, or these people, or this case."

"I don't either. But I'm not going to throw it up till its solved. One of these nice-mannered customers has done the old boy in, and we're going to find out which. You're probably worried because you don't think it's the sort of story for you to write up. You've always done nice cheerful murders, haven't you? You try your hand at this, though. It may be nasty, but it's very, very promising. I've got the beginnings of an idea already."

"You don't feel an air of danger?"

"Not yet, I don't. But I shouldn't be surprised if there wasn't a bit of funny work if I find out too much. You just watch."

5

After dinner I accompanied Beef to the little sitting-room beyond the kitchen which was occupied by the Gabriels. It was cosy and very warm with a table covered with a red plush table-cloth, a loud-ticking clock and an apparently comatose tortoiseshell cat on the hearth.

Mrs. Gabriel, a little sharp-featured and as we found sharp-tongued woman, was introduced and Beef was given the large armchair by the fire while I was shown a wooden kitchen chair at the table.

Beef did not seem in a hurry to come to the point, and when he had been handed an enormous cup of dark brown tea into which four or five spoonfuls of sugar had been stirred by Mrs. Gabriel, he started to comment on the row of photographs beside him.

"Yes, that's my daughter's wedding," said Mrs. Gabriel as Beef held a framed postcard. "She was a picture, wasn't she?"

I could see a group of people looking as though they were being mesmerized by a boa-constrictor and made no comment.

"Lovely!" said Beef.

"And that's my boy. He's in the Navy."

The information was scarcely necessary, for Gabriel Junior was in uniform. He was grinning like a ventriloquist's dummy.

Beef took a long gulp from his cup.

"Very nice," he said, and even I could not decide whether he meant the tea or the sailor. "Well now…"

"You want to know all about this business don't you, Sarge?" asked Gabriel, a little too glibly, I thought. "Well, you shall hear what we know. And that's more than the police have done. What do you want me to tell you?"

"Who you think did it, first of all."

Like many of Beef's questions this seemed to be unexpected.

"Well…" said Gabriel.

"It's very hard to say…" reflected Mrs. Gabriel.

"If you had to make a guess?" persisted Beef.

"It looks very black against young Rudolf, yet I don't somehow think it was him. Not the type, really. Too happy-go-lucky. I can't really imagine who it might have been," said Gabriel.

"Unless…" began his wife.

"I know what she's going to say. You take this with a pinch of salt, Sarge. She's prejudiced."

"Oh no I'm not. I'll tell you who my guess is, though it's only a guess. Alice Dunton. That's who."

"What makes you think that?"

"Because she's a proper she-devil, that's why. She threatened me with a hatchet once when she worked here, and I've heard her breathing fire against the old man."

"Why?"

"Because it was through him she was sacked, and then Dunton wouldn't go with her."

"But is there any reason to think she was in the grounds that night?"

"Not that I know of. That's my guess, all the same."

There was a pause and Beef studied his notebook.

"If Rudolf had nothing to do with it what was he doing out in the grounds at that time?"

The Gabriels looked at him in amazement.

"Do you mean to say you don't know?" said Mrs. Gabriel.

"You're not pulling my leg?" asked her husband.

Beef protested his innocence.

"He'd been with Her," explained Gabriel shortly but obscurely.

"You mean?"

"Of course. Been going on for months. Mrs. Ducrow would go up to bed at nine or ten and before midnight he was in her room. Every night. They might have been a married couple. Even the police suspect that, I believe."

"So that's what they're all trying to keep dark? You surprise me. When Dunton saw him he was just going home then?"

"That's it."

Mrs. Gabriel spoke with something like a hiss of malice in her voice.

"You wouldn't think it, would you? Young chap, too. She must be over forty. But you can see it if you look at her. It's written in her face. Soon as ever I saw her I knew what she was."

"This must strengthen the case against Rudolf," reflected Beef. "Gives him an extra motive. Did the old man know anything about it?"

"Him? Certainly not. He wouldn't see it however much under his nose it was, unless someone told him about it. Mind you if he *had* known there'd have been ructions. He wouldn't have taken that lying down. He thought the world of her. Proper silly about her, he was, and always had been. They say there's no fool like an old one. You'd go a long way before you'd find anyone more in love with his wife than what he was."

"Do you agree?" Beef asked Gabriel.

"Oh, yes. No two ways about it. We'd remarked on it a hundred times."

"So if he did find out?"

"Well, he hadn't at dinner-time, that's a sure thing. He wasn't one who could hide it when he was upset, and at dinner that evening he was as cheerful as you please. If he did find out it was later that evening."

"Then you think he might have..."

"Might have done anything. He was only a weak little chap, but I wouldn't put anything past him if he found that out."

"That's very interesting," said Beef.

"Though mind you," put in Mrs. Gabriel rather spitefully. "I'd blame *her* as much as Rudolf if that is what happened. You know about her drinking, don't you? Bottles and bottles she gets through in her room on her own. I've seen her so that she could scarcely stand."

"Mind you, Rudolf helped her with that," said Gabriel.

"I daresay," his wife went on. "The funny thing is the old man knew about her drinking and was very worried about it, but he never had a hint of the other."

"Did either of you hear anything that night?"

Mrs. Gabriel smiled rather cruelly.

"Hear anything? I should say we did. Our room is at the top of the back stairs, and there's no carpet down. You can hear anyone coming up or down that way."

"So you heard Rudolf, for instance?"

"We were used to that. As a matter of fact we used to leave the back door open for him. We heard him go up just before midnight."

"Then?"

"Then about quarter of an hour later someone else came up the back stairs. I thought of waking Gabriel, but he'd only just dropped off, after coughing all the evening. I wondered if it was someone who had come in at the back door but I thought it was no business of mine."

"Was that all?"

"No. A few minutes later two of them went downstairs, again by the back way."

"You're sure? Two?"

"Certain. I heard them, though they were going quietly. I went to sleep after that but Gabriel had me awake again in the early morning. Not long after five, it must have been. He had a terrible hacking cough and kept on and on till it nearly drove me mad. When I heard the clock strike a quarter past five and knew we only had another two hours' rest, I decided to get up and find him something for it. I was just going to switch on the lights when I heard a car coming up the drive. I was curious and went across to the window to have a look. I could see the headlights coming towards the house, then the car was pulled up rather sharp."

"Where would it have been then?"

"It's hard to say. I think it had just turned the bend before the summer-house, but I can't be sure. It stopped there for quite a few minutes with its headlights on."

"Couldn't you see where they were shining?"

"Not really. They seemed to be almost towards me. Then they were switched off and only sidelights left on."

"Have you told the police this?"

"Certainly not. Let them find out. After a bit I heard the engine start up and then I couldn't follow what was happening, but I think the car was either backed away or turned.

After a bit I could hear it going down the drive towards the lodge gates."

"Did you hear it all?" Beef asked Gabriel.

"Not really. I had a sort of idea in the morning when she told me, but no more than that."

"You've no idea whether it was a big powerful car or a little one?"

"Not really, though I have a sort of idea it was big."

"What cars are there in the family?"

"Quite a few. Mr. Rudolf's got a Jaguar. Mr. Gray's is an Austin saloon. Major Gulley has an old Lagonda. Then there's Mr. Ducrow's Daimler, which was scarcely ever used, and Mrs. Ducrow's Hillman Minx."

"Who looks after them all?"

"The chauffeur. Young Mills. Well, I say young; he must be thirty now."

"Decent chap?"

"He's all right. Keeps to himself."

"So anyone of them could have been driving that car, or someone not of the family at all?"

"That's right."

"What about the lodge gates?"

"They were kept permanently open then. It's only since Mr. Ducrow's death they're shut. Reporters and that—there was no peace at all. It was the police recommended it."

Beef, pondered, then seemed satisfied.

"You've been most helpful, both of you."

"'Nother cup of tea?" suggested Mrs. Gabriel.

Beef agreed.

"That changes things somewhat," he said. "But I daresay we shall get round it. Now is there anything else you can tell me while I'm here?"

"There's one other thing," went on Mrs. Gabriel, "but I don't know if it's worth mentioning. There's a little cloakroom in the hall where all the men's coats are hung. The police spent a whole morning there looking at every coat in the place and taking them away after, and goodness knows what. But one thing they didn't see because it wasn't there."

"And what was that?"

"An old jacket of Rudolf's. It had hung there for weeks. Goodness knows how it came to be here instead of in his own house. Must have taken it off in the summer and gone home without it. Anyway, there it hung. But on the morning after the murder it had gone."

"Now whatever made you notice that?" asked Beef.

"Just chance, really. I knew there were some matches in the pocket and I wanted to light a cigarette. I know I did that the morning before. But when I came to it that day it had vanished. I looked carefully among the coats. Not a sign."

"It may or may not be important," pronounced Beef. "Now I think we better go through to them in the drawing-room. I'm most obliged to you both."

"That's all right, Sarge," said Gabriel. "Anything we can do."

I reflected how much at home Beef was with people like the Gabriels and how they always seemed to fall over themselves to help him. If only he could get the truth out of more educated people as quickly, what a detective he would be!

As soon as we entered the drawing-room that sense of overhanging danger returned to me. The three people there were too much posed. It was as though they had been set in their places by a clever producer. Mrs. Ducrow was doing some embroidery, and although when I examined it I realized that it was very good work indeed, yet it seemed out of place in her hands. Gulley was reading *The Field* and Gray

The Letters of Gertrude Bell. It all looked too arranged, though Beef could scarcely have guessed this.

They could not, however, restrain themselves from staring anxiously at Beef.

"How did you get on?" asked Gulley.

"Not bad," said Beef. "I've got a long way to go. I can see that."

"Wouldn't they talk?" persisted Gulley.

"Oh, yes, they talked. But it doesn't add up to anything yet."

"Pity," said Gulley. "We're all beginning to feel the strain a bit. And for Rudolf it must be appalling."

"I'll do my best," said Beef, "if everyone will help."

"I'm sure we'll do that."

"Then can any of you tell me whose car was driven up the drive at five o'clock that morning?"

This was clearly as much of a bombshell as Beef had hoped. Gulley appeared like a whiskered fish. Mrs. Ducrow stared down at her embroidery, and Gray looked frankly amazed.

"A car?" he said. "What kind of car?"

"Large," said Beef. "Know whose it was?"

But none of them seemed able to make even a guess at that.

6

I was relieved to find that there was a key in the lock of my bedroom door. I was firmly convinced that there was a murderer in that gloomy house or in one of its lodges, and it had occurred to me that he might not be sane. In that case no one was safe. However, during that first night nothing happened to disturb me.

At breakfast we were four men, Mrs. Ducrow not appearing. Beef asked if he might be shown the exact spot in which Cosmo Ducrow's body had been found by Dunton, and Gulley agreed to take us there. Gray was going to fetch Rudolf Ducrow in case Beef was ready to see him later in the morning.

It was a cold windy morning, but the rain which had been falling in the night had ceased now. Beef suggested that we should leave the house by the french windows in the library, thus following the route which, presumably, the murdered man had taken.

We stepped out on to a flagged terrace and Gulley explained the lay of the land. We walked by a well-defined grass path to some wrought-iron gates which divided the garden proper from the grassy parkland beyond. This, we learnt, was let as grazing to a local farmer, but a tennis court and croquet lawn were fenced off from it at about two hundred yards from the house.

"There used to be a cricket ground for the village club, here," said Gulley, "but Cosmo did away with that. He did not like intruders. It caused some bad feeling at first, I gather, but Theo Gray persuaded him to buy another ground for the local team and have it levelled for them. That is on the other side of the village. What was the pavilion here we use as a summer-house and keep the croquet mallets and things in it."

We were now crossing the rough grass and approaching the wire fence. This was a simple one with two strands of wire only, put up to keep the cattle from the tennis court and croquet lawn but easily passed through by any human being. We followed Gulley into the enclosure.

"We've come just 335 paces from the house," remarked Beef. "Where was the body found?"

Gulley led us to a metal and wooden seat such as one sees in public parks. This was within the enclosure, about ten yards from the little pavilion.

"Cosmo was lying here," he said. "Just beside this seat."

Beef made a great show of looking about him in every direction.

"Is that the drive we came up yesterday?" he asked, pointing to a tarmac road a few yards away.

Gulley seemed less interested in this.

"Yes. That's one of the drives," he said shortly. "The body lay here."

"Is it the main drive from the lodge gates to the house?"

"Yes."

"Then why do you say one of the drives? Where's the other?"

"There is a way for tradesmen's vans from another gate to the back of the house."

"But if a private car were coming up to the house it would take this one?"

"I suppose so."

"Now exactly where was the body?"

"I can't say to within a foot. Somewhere by this seat."

Gulley seemed to keep on the croquet lawn side of the seat, but Beef was examining something on the side nearer the drive.

"I see there's two pegs in here," he said, "about five foot apart. They look as though they had been put in by the police to mark the exact position of the cadaver."

I would have been amused at Beef's use of this word if I had not been so interested in the reactions of Major Gulley to Beef's suggestion. He was clearly put out and nervous.

"Very likely," he said huffily.

"You're not sure?"

"I've told you what I think."

"Supposing this to have been the position of the corpse, I should like to see when it would come into view from the drive."

Gulley stared angrily at him as Beef went to the pavilion and brought out two croquet hoops which he drove into the ground at the two peg-holes. He then marched down the drive and began to walk towards us. The drive had a fairly sharp bend at about this point, and it was as Beef rounded this that he stopped.

"About here, I should think," he said and stood looking towards us.

"I don't see what you're getting at," said Gulley.

"Just supposition," Beef replied airily. "Just supposition about that car. Now let's have a look at the croquet hammers."

"Mallets. The police have taken the one used, of course. That was Rudolf's special one."

"Did I understand yesterday that you each had one?"

"Not really. The rest of us used any one that came handy. Hallo!"

Major Gulley was staring at the croquet mallets leaning against the wall. He then began to search the pavilion.

"That's very odd," he said and I was convinced that he was genuinely surprised. "That's very odd indeed. One is missing."

"You just said that the police..."

"No, no. There were six altogether. The police have Rudolf's, but there are only four here."

"Sure?"

"Absolutely."

"When did you see them all last?"

"Last time we played. Back in September."

"Perhaps the gardener might have used it for something?"

"Very unlikely. He has a perfectly good mallet and a sledge-hammer."

"Is it any particular one?"

"No. I don't think so."

Beef appeared to lose interest in the missing mallet, and returned to the drive.

"Of course," he said, "it's a fortnight ago, so if a car did turn here the wheel-marks would scarcely be showing now. Or any other marks, for that matter. I came into this case too late."

"Too late for what?" asked Gulley.

"Too late to clear young Rudolf Ducrow."

"You'd better tell him that yourself. This is Rudolf coming up from his cottage now with Theo Gray."

I was favourably impressed by Rudolf as soon as I saw that he had frank blue eyes, a rather Anglo-Saxon sort of face, and an open breezy manner. Beef, however, seemed more reserved.

"Come down to save my bacon?" said Rudolf cheerfully.

"Well, you've got your work cut out for you. This thing looks so black for me that I can't understand why I haven't been arrested."

"I don't understand that, either," said Beef. "But I know Inspector Stute who is in charge of the case, and I daresay I shall find out from him." Beef then looked very steadily at Rudolf and asked in steady tones: "Did you do it?"

"Oddly enough, I didn't. I liked the old boy. He was crackers, I suppose. Misanthropic and so on. But you couldn't dislike him. And in any case I don't want to kill anyone again."

"Rudolf was a Commando," put in Gulley.

"I see. You knew that you would be a rich man in case of your uncle's death?"

"I had all I wanted. Cosmo gave me a couple of thousand a year free of tax."

"You're very frank, Mr. Ducrow."

"I've got to be. You're my last hope, they tell me."

"I'm not holding out any hope at present," said Beef. "I don't know enough about it. But we'll have a talk on our own later. I'll try to put the truth together, somehow."

"All right."

"Now, is that where the body lay?"

"Yes. Exactly."

"When did you see it there?"

"When Dunton called me over in the morning."

"Had you passed this spot during the night?"

A little pause.

"Very near it."

"But you saw nothing?"

"No."

"How many of these croquet mallets were kept here?"

"Six."

"When did you see them last?"

"To notice them, about a month ago when Dunton was putting all the hoops away for the winter."

"And you, Mr. Gray?"

"I think when we last played."

"There's one missing besides the one the police have got."

"Oh?"

"Is this pavilion ever locked?"

"No. We don't bother."

"Thank you, Mr. Ducrow. We'll go into the rest presently. Perhaps I could call on you this afternoon? Now may we go back to the house?"

Rudolf, after telling Beef to come any time after lunch, left us and the four of us started on our way back to the terrace.

"There's only one man now I haven't seen," reflected Beef, "that's Mills, the chauffeur. Mind if I go round to the garage now?"

"By all means," said Gulley. "But you won't find Mills very talkative."

"That's what I was told about Gabriel," Beef retorted and for some reason this silenced Gulley.

But at first it seemed that Gulley was right. Mills was a tall thin young man, shifty-eyed and tight-lipped. Nor was Beef's blunt approach calculated to draw much information from him.

"What do you know about this business?" Beef asked.

"Only what I'm told."

"Where were you that night?"

"In bed and asleep."

"Where's your room?"

"Over the garage."

"What cars were out at the time?"

"Only Major Gulley's. He was in London."

"When did he get back?"

"About eleven o'clock next morning."

"Anything else to tell me?"

Mills seemed to be sizing Beef up, deciding whether to be frank or not.

"Yes," he said at last. "It's about Gulley's car. I keep my own records of distances travelled with all these cars. I was in REME during the war, see? Force of habit. When Gulley got back on the morning after the murder his speedometer showed that he'd done just about twice the distance he should have if he had just been to London and back."

"Very interesting. Does anyone know you do that?"

"No."

"You might keep it up, will you? This is going to be a tricky case for me, and every little bit of information helps. All the cars are kept here, are they?"

"All except Rudolf Ducrow's. He keeps his down at his place."

"Has he got a garage there?"

"No. Just puts a tarpaulin over it in bad weather, otherwise leaves it out."

Beef's glance had been going upward while we talked and he now pointed to the roof.

"It looks as though one could get out there," he said.

"Yes. You can."

"And from there anyone could see the whole place, right down to the lodge gates, I suppose?"

"Yes. I think so."

"Do you know the way up?"

"Yes. I'll take you."

"All right. You go and join the rest of them," Beef said to me. "Tell them I'm talking to Mills here. You can pile it on a bit about my interest in that car without saying anything about Gulley's speedometer. Any mention of that car seems to shake them, doesn't? Some of them anyhow."

"I'll see whether it can be done naturally," I said.

I watched the two of them going towards the house, the tall sinewy chauffeur and Beef, looking I suddenly perceived, rather out of condition. A thought sprang to my mind and I called Beef back.

"Be careful," I whispered, "he's a powerful chap. We don't know he's not the murderer, do we?"

"You mean well," said Beef, "but you do say some silly things sometimes."

Then he followed Mills to the back door.

I found everyone gathered in the library, and as I entered there was a sudden silence while they stared enquiringly at me. I saw that Mrs. Ducrow had joined them and thought she was looking flushed and excited. Rudolf was stretched out in a chair smoking a pipe. It was Gray who broke the silence.

"Where is Sergeant Beef?" he asked, attempting to sound pleasant.

"He has been talking to Mills," I told them. "He seems particularly interested in the matter of the car. Now Mills has taken him up so that he can see the whole disposition of the ground from the roof." I decided to end with a little joke. "Le boeuf sur le toit!" I said. But nobody laughed.

7

Lunch was an embarrassing meal because it was now obvious to everyone that Mrs. Ducrow had been drinking too much. She was not intoxicated, but there was an unnatural animation about her and she laughed once or twice for very little reason.

When we had finished the meal she turned to Beef.

"I would like you to come to the drawing-room," she said. "There is something I want to discuss."

Gulley looked perturbed and said: "Wouldn't it be better for you to see Beef this evening, Freda? He has arranged to go down to the lodge and interview Rudolf. What do you think, Theo?"

Gray seemed undecided and Mrs. Ducrow assumed her grandest manner.

"I shall see him now," she announced, and led the way to her beautifully furnished drawing-room. Beef looked out of place among the delicate Sheraton furniture and Bow pottery, but he sat down quietly and waited for Mrs. Ducrow to speak.

"There is something you ought to know," she said. "It may alter the entire case. It is not easy for me to discuss it, and I could not bring myself to tell the police. But too much seems to depend on it now for me to remain silent."

"Before you tell me this," said Beef, "I ought to warn you that whatever it is I may not be able to keep it to myself. If it is vital information I could not help giving it to the police. Otherwise I should become an accessory after the fact."

"I realize that. You must do as you think right. The truth is that Rudolf was with me that night. We have been... lovers for more than a year. He would never have told you this himself, bless him. He is the sort of man who would... face trial before he would implicate a woman."

Beef nodded solemnly but said nothing. Mrs. Ducrow seemed puzzled and put out by his silence.

"You realize what this means?" she said. "It explains what he was doing in the park that morning. He had left me to walk home."

"That is so. But it also provides an additional motive for murder."

She grew a little hysterical now.

"Why do you say that?" she almost shouted. "He didn't murder Cosmo. He would never have done such a thing. Why should he?"

"Take it easy now," said Beef, trying to sound comforting in his rough way. "It won't help if you lose your head. And you must see why it was an additional motive. He is in love with you, Mrs. Ducrow."

"What of it?"

"A man in love makes plans. What he wanted was to marry you."

"But his wife..."

"With the money he would inherit from his uncle he could soon arrange a settlement and divorce from her. Now I'm not saying he did it. I'm only saying that what you have told me cuts both ways."

"If anything happens to him I shall kill myself."

Beef looked very grave.

"That's one thing you must *not* say. Ever."

"I shall! You'll see! If anything happens to Rudy I shall kill myself."

Beef was at a loss. His experience had failed to teach him what to do in such a case.

"I want a little more information," he said uneasily.

Freda Ducrow at once seemed to pull herself together and to look at Beef suspiciously.

"Well?"

"His wife must have known about this. How did she take it?"

"You will meet her presently and perhaps understand. She is a strange woman. She seems to care for nothing but dogs and horses. She never loved Rudy though I think she loved the prospect of money. As long as she could have that, and freedom to ride and breed dogs and so on, she did not seem to care. Of course she knew he came here at night."

"And your husband?"

I think her expression softened.

"He had no inkling," she said. "He was a good man and trusted everyone. If he had guessed anything of the sort we should all have known instantly. He could not keep things to himself. No, he never had any idea, unless..."

"Unless?"

"Well, something rather strange did happen that evening. Rudy used to come in by the back door and up the back staircase past the Gabriels' bedroom. They... I'm afraid they knew he used to come to me and left the back door open for him. But that night as Rudy came into the kitchen he noticed that the door leading from the kitchen to the main hall was ajar. This was unusual but he would not have taken any more notice if he had not turned round just as he was about to go up the back stairs. When he looked the door was shut. It was as though someone was watching him.

"He supposed that it was Gabriel. But as he passed the Gabriels' bedroom he heard them talking together. He did not go down again but told me about it. I did not take it very seriously. It seemed unthinkable that it should be Cosmo."

"I see. Now from the time you said good night to him and Mr. Gray at ten o'clock that evening you never saw your husband alive again?"

"No."

"At what time did Rudolf Ducrow come to your room?"

"At about midnight, I think."

"And remained till?"

"Till we heard the clock strike four."

"You heard no sound from outside during that time?"

"No. But some minutes after he had left me I heard Theo Gray pass my door. I waited for his return and he told me that he had heard shouts in the grounds and had phoned to Dunton to be on the look-out."

"So it was possible, in point of time I mean, for Rudolf to have caused those shouts?"

"I suppose so. I'm glad I've managed to tell you all this, Sergeant. I feel I can trust you. Of course, both Theo and Gulley have been very kind but they're so worried themselves. I have thought of going to see my old family solicitor down at Folkover. But I'm sure you can clear Rudy of this terrible thing."

"If he's not guilty he will be cleared," said Beef solemnly. "One more thing. What was he wearing that night?"

"I can't be sure. He very rarely wore an overcoat, though. Probably a sports coat of some kind and flannel trousers. Why? Is it important?"

"It may be very important," said Beef. "Now you take my advice and go and have forty winks. Do you good when you're upset like that. I'm going to see Rudolf Ducrow this afternoon, then maybe I'll have better news for you."

It was strange to see that big masterful woman look like an admonished child.

"But... I haven't told you the most important thing of all," she said. "At least I think it is. It happened at about eleven o'clock, soon after I had heard Theo go up to bed for the first time. My room faces east, as you know, and looks out over the terrace. My window was open a little at the top. I heard a whistle."

"A whistle? But Mrs. Ducrow it was a gusty night. How could you have heard a whistle from up in your room?"

"I don't mean a low, secret sort of whistle. It was a special shrill whistle repeated in a certain way."

"You had heard it before?"

"Oh yes, often. I knew it quite well. It was the whistle used by Zena Ducrow to call those dogs of hers. Rudolf's wife, I mean."

"And where do you suppose she was when she whistled?"

"Not far away. It sounded almost as though she was on the terrace."

"Did she often come up to the house?"

"Not very often. She and Cosmo did not get on very well."

The crude attempts at gentleness seemed to have gone out of Beef's manner now. He did not again suggest that Mrs. Ducrow should go and lie down but said brusquely that he was going to see Rudolf, and left the room.

"Is he really clever?" Mrs. Ducrow asked me. "Will he find out the truth?"

"He always has done," I said confidently.

"I couldn't go on living without Rudy. I couldn't!"

I showed my tactfulness and resource.

"The clouds will soon go by," I said, and with a reassuring smile to her I hurried after Beef.

As we were pulling on our coats Theo Gray came up.

"There's something I should like you to do, Beef, if you would. Not a piece of investigation but something practical and helpful."

"If it conforms..." began Beef, but Gray spoke rather urgently.

"Rudolf has a gun in his house," he said. "A twelve-bore. I think that in the circumstances it would be much wiser if just now he was relieved of it."

"Why?"

"It's a lethal weapon, you know. However much Rudolf seems to be bearing up under all this it must be a terrible strain."

"You mean he might..."

"I don't know. I just think it would be better if he had not got it down there."

"You may be right. I'll see what I can do."

"Thank you. I may be exaggerating the danger, of course. But Rudolf is not quite the carefree young man he appears."

"Where does he keep it?"

"I don't know, I'm afraid. But you can soon find out."

We started walking down the drive, and as I guessed he would, Beef began to reflect aloud on the results of his investigations so far.

"*You* ought to be pleased," he said. "Just the job for you. Suspect under every stone. There wasn't one of them who doesn't seem to have been around the house that night."

"Except Major Gulley," I pointed out.

Beef let out a roar of laughter but made no other answer.

"I thought it wouldn't be long before someone brought in Rudolf's wife."

We had reached the point where the drive ran nearest to the little fenced-off area kept for tennis and croquet, and Beef stopped and looked towards the pavilion. With a curt command to me to follow he walked across and opened the door, then stood looking down at the mallets and balls.

"Come on," he said presently. "You'n me are going to have a basinful of this."

"What on earth do you mean?"

"Game of croquet, of course. Get hold of those hoops."

I pointed out to Beef that we were visible from the house and that it would be in the worst possible taste to do anything of the sort.

"Taste?" he said. "You forget that there's been a murder here. That wasn't in such wonderful taste, was it? Now show us where these hoops go."

Nothing would satisfy him till we had set out the appurtenances of the game. He commented caustically on it, maintaining that it was not a patch on darts, then tried to wield his mallet. I have no particular skill at croquet but I found it easy to do better than Beef, whose game was clumsy in the extreme. He kept swinging his mallet as though he were playing golf and using a driver. But something was on his mind as he did so, and when I asked him sarcastically whether this was a necessary part of his investigation he replied with a rather distasteful Americanism: "What do you think?" he asked.

Then, keeping on the side of the pavilion farthest from the house so that he was invisible from its windows, he began to swing the mallet in the air in the most extraordinary way, chopping it downward on an imaginary mark. I could guess the object of this manoeuvre and asked him whether a woman could have wielded the mallet which had killed Cosmo Ducrow.

He looked at me in his bland innocent way then said, "A woman was just as capable of it as a man."

Finally he helped me replace all the articles in the pavilion and began to walk on towards the two lodges.

"Now I *am* getting somewhere," he said. "Now I am beginning to see daylight."

I am accustomed to these cryptic statements of his and knowing that if I asked any questions he would only grow more obscure, I said nothing.

8

Rudolf came to the door of the lodge in which he lived and invited us in, explaining that his wife was out.

"Pity," said Beef, "I'd like a few words with her."

"With Zena? Oh, I suppose Mrs. Ducrow has told you that story of hers about hearing Zena whistling the dogs. Imagination, if you ask me."

"Where was your wife that night, Mr. Ducrow?"

"She went to the pictures. Took the car. It really won't help you to try to involve her, I assure you."

"Everyone is involved," said Beef. "And now we've got to do some very plain talking. I may as well tell you at once that Mrs. Ducrow has told me where you were that night. And other nights."

Rudolf stood up. I thought at first that he was going to be violently angry, but after a few moments' silence he spoke in a tense but well-controlled voice.

"She shouldn't have done that."

"It had to come out. I shall be surprised if the police don't know. And at least it explains what you were doing in the park at four o'clock in the morning."

He remained thoughtful.

"Tell me about that evening."

As he told his story I for one believed that Rudolf was speaking the truth. He told of the open door in the kitchen which had mysteriously and silently closed when he started going up the back stairs; he confirmed Freda Ducrow's estimate of the time of his leaving her; he said that during his walk home he had neither seen nor heard anything unusual. He had left the house by the back door as usual, come round to the front and followed the drive. It had taken him perhaps six or seven minutes because he had to go very quietly out of the house and silently shut the door after him. He had passed near the pavilion, as he always did on his way down the drive, but had noticed nothing. He had been very surprised to see Dunton waiting about near the lodges. When he got in he went straight up to bed. His wife always slept with her door open, and as he passed her room he heard her snoring. He knew nothing more. It was true that the bloodstained croquet mallet found by the body was his favourite and was used by no one else. He knew that he and Freda Ducrow and Theo Gray were equal beneficiaries under Cosmo's will. He agreed that the case looked black against him, but he was innocent.

"There were no lights showing in the lower windows of the house that night when you left?"

"No."

"You didn't hear a car pass through the lodge gates after you got to bed?"

"No."

"You've nothing else to tell me about that night?"

"Nothing. So far as I knew till the morning it was a night like any other. There was just that half-open door. Oh, and one other thing, though it obviously has nothing to do with Cosmo's death."

"Well?"

"I was alone in this house all the evening until I went up to Hokestones about midnight. Some time after ten one of my wife's dogs started barking and I went out to see what was disturbing the creature. She breeds Boxers, you know, and she trains them not to make a racket unless they're disturbed. This one barked for about two minutes. I took a torch and went to the kennels. Just as I was returning I saw what had disturbed the dog. Someone was standing outside Dunton's front door."

"His wife, I suppose?"

"Yes. But she had not been near the place for weeks and had left Dunton because he stayed with Cosmo. She saw me and asked if I knew whether Dunton was in. I said that as far as I knew he was, and just then the door was opened by Dunton and they went in together."

"It only needed that," said Beef. "That means there were at least a dozen people round the place at one time or another that night."

"Good Lord, you surely don't suppose that Mrs. Dunton could have had anything to do with it?"

"But who could? That's what I want to know. No one can believe that anyone else would do such a thing. But he didn't crack his own head open with a croquet mallet. Now suppose it was Cosmo Ducrow at the kitchen door. Suppose he saw you going upstairs to his wife's bedroom. What would he have done?"

"I don't know, but something pretty desperate. He wouldn't have let it pass."

"What anyone might *suppose* he did was to wait till you came down, follow you across the park to the pavilion and there attack you in some way which would make you strike in self-defence..."

"No," said Rudolf, "that wouldn't work. You can't smash the back of a man's skull in with a croquet mallet in self-defence. Besides, as I've told you, I never saw him that evening at all."

"All right," said Beef wearily. "Let's leave it at that, shall we? I was going to ask you whether you've by any chance got an old gun you could lend me? If there's one thing I enjoy it's a bit of rabbit-shooting, and there should be plenty round the park."

Rudolf smiled.

"I'll lend you my gun," he said, "but you needn't be afraid I'm going to do myself in. Or anyone else, for that matter."

"Still with all this going on you'd be better with it out of the way," said Beef. "Where is it?"

Rudolf rose and led the way to a little cloakroom. It was not more than ten feet square and was part of the house which had been built on, I surmised. Besides the W.C. there was a hand-basin, a row of coat pegs with overcoats hanging from them, and an old table on which were a dog's comb and brush, while under it were three dog-baskets. The whole room smelt of dogs.

Rudolf explained that some of his wife's Boxers slept here and added that they were all over the place. Then he pointed to his gun, which was leaning against the wall by the laden coat pegs. Beef went across to pick it up, but before doing so he stopped and stood staring at the coats. Then he turned to Rudolf.

"Is this your jacket?" he asked casually.

Rudolf did not seem interested.

"Yes; an old one," he said.

"Why do you keep it down here with the overcoats?"

"I didn't know it was here."

"Where is it usually kept?"

"Upstairs, I suppose. I haven't worn it for some time."

"Mr. Ducrow, I would ask you to try to remember everything you can about this jacket. I regard it as important. When did you wear it last?"

"I can't say, really. Back in the summer, I think."

"You were not wearing it on the night of the murder?"

"No... well, I don't think so. I can't remember when I wore it."

"You have another light-coloured sports coat?"

"Yes. Two. This is the oldest."

"Have you ever hung this up in the house—at Hokestones, I mean?"

Light broke on Rudolf's face.

"Why, yes. Now you mention it. I remember leaving it up there in the summer. I was going to do a job on the car with Mills and went out in my shirt sleeves. Then I drove straight here, forgetting it altogether."

"Did you never go and fetch it?"

"No. Clean forgot."

"How did it get here then?"

"Blowed if I know."

"Come now, Mr. Ducrow. There must be some explanation."

"I don't know. I may have brought it down, but I can't remember doing so."

"How long has it been here?"

"Don't know that either, I'm afraid. Never noticed it before."

"Do you mind if I take it away with me?"

Rudolf smiled.

"To wear for rabbit-shooting? All right."

Beef picked up the gun and jacket, and laden with these we were making for the front door when there was a fury of barking outside and we heard a woman's deep voice, shouting, "Down, Stalin! Come here, Molotov! Lenin, will you behave yourself?" Then a loud shrill whistle repeated four times on one note: Whee, WHEE, whee, WHEEEE. The front door opened and a pack of Boxers hurtled in followed by a hefty young woman in jodhpurs. The dogs barked and sniffed round us, but without animosity. There was a scene of much confusion till their names had been shouted again and the whole of the Supreme Soviet had been incarcerated in the cloakroom.

"My wife," explained Rudolf unnecessarily.

Zena gave a painful handshake to each of us and boomed, "Better have a cup of tea before you go," adding to Rudolf, "That's the least you can do if they're going to save your skin."

Beef, I could see, did not much relish this light-hearted treatment of the matter in hand, but came back into the sitting-room with us. It was Rudolf who went out to the kitchen, and this gave Beef an opportunity to put one of his embarrassingly direct questions to Zena.

"Were you up at the house on the night of the murder?"

After only a few seconds' pause she grinned.

"Yes. I wonder how you discovered that. I didn't think anyone saw me except Cosmo."

"Oh, he did?"

"Of course. I went to see him. I knew he'd be in the library and went straight to the french windows."

"What did you want to see him about?"

"Don't you know? You know about Rudolf and Freda, don't you?" Beef nodded. "Well, old Cosmo and I were the wronged parties, as it were. I thought we ought to get together and make some decisions."

"And did you?"

"Extraordinary thing. The old boy wouldn't believe a word of it. I never dreamt he wasn't wise to the whole thing. Everyone else was—even the servants. But no, he wouldn't believe it. Shook him—I could see that. But he would not admit it was possible."

"At what time was this?"

"Not late. Soon after eleven, I should think."

"Did you offer any proof?"

"I told him he could find them together any night. It seemed just silly to me, his refusing to face facts."

"How long were you with him?"

"About half an hour, I should think."

"And you left him in the library?"

"Well, he was walking about as I talked to him and when I left I saw him go towards the door."

"Did you come straight home?"

"No. I didn't want to meet Rudy on his way to Freda. *Too* embarrassing. So I slunk off by the back drive and came round by the road."

"Have you told the police this?"

"Good Lord, no. I don't want to get involved, and anyway it would make things worse for Rudy, wouldn't it? There's no grudge between us, you know. Just don't like being married to one another. If I said that I'd just shown Cosmo the light on Rudy and Freda it would suggest that there might have been some sort of a showdown between uncle and nephew, don't you think?"

"And you don't think there was?"

"No. Rudy says he didn't see the old boy that night. He's a dirty dog in some ways, but he doesn't lie."

"Do you, Mrs. Ducrow?"

"Like a trooper. But I've told you the truth about this."

Rudolf Ducrow came in with a tray. We drank tea without speaking much except for a few questions from Beef to Zena about the jacket. She had never noticed it, she said, or noticed its absence lately. She had sometimes worn it herself last winter when she was going out to feed the dogs.

"Do you play this game of croquet?" Beef asked finally.

"Don't be a chump!" bellowed Zena. "Dam' silly kids game. What do you take me for? I'll give you a game of snooker if you want it."

Without accepting this invitation and still carrying coat and gun, Beef took his leave.

9

We came out of the cold little house and smell of dogs into darkness, but Beef did not start walking towards Hokestones. He hesitated a minute then announced his intention of paying a call on Dunton. I remembered the big surly fellow who had so grudgingly opened the gates for us yesterday and it seemed to me that the interview would be a difficult one. I thought of returning to the house and leaving Beef to make this visit alone. With that annoying faculty he has for guessing one's thoughts, Beef sensed my hesitation.

"No need for you to come if you don't want to," he said. "I'll tell you afterwards if he says anything worth hearing."

"I'll come," I retorted, deciding not to be put off by Beef.

"He can't eat you, after all," Beef pointed out.

There was no answer to our first knock, and we stood in the cold and darkness listening for some sound from within. At last, when we had knocked again rather loudly, we heard steps in the passage and after bolts had been pulled back and a key turned the door opened. We could see the outline of Dunton's great bulk, but he had apparently closed the door of the room which he had left, for there was no light behind him.

"Oh, it's you," he growled, and I thought he sounded relieved. "Well, what do you want?"

"To interrogate you," said Beef.

"I've got nothing to say."

"That's for me to judge. Now there's no good in you being awkward about this, Dunton. I've got my duty to do."

"Ask me what you want then, and hurry up about it. I won't stand here all night for you, or anyone else."

"Nor won't I!" said Beef, as usual growing ungrammatical with exasperation. "So you might just as well ask us in."

"You ask what you want here."

"I know you've got your wife back with you so that's no reason to keep us all shivering here."

"You... What the hell have you..."

"Now come along, come along," said Beef as though he were gently clearing a crowd from a street accident. "We might just as well get this over. I may want to ask your wife one or two things, too."

Dunton still hesitated for a moment then suddenly turned and led the way down the short passage.

"Shut the door after you," he said.

The light in his kitchen was quite dazzling for a moment, then I saw a strange-looking woman standing by the stove. Mrs. Dunton was scraggy and untidy-looking; thick dark hair, turning to grey, was loosely tied and her eyes were resentful and rather wild, I thought. She said nothing as we entered, answering Beef's hearty "Good evening" with a nod.

"Now what do you want?" asked Dunton.

Beef held up the jacket he had found in Rudolf's cloak-room.

"Is this what he was wearing?"

"How the hell should I know? I'm woken up at four o'clock in the morning to go out and look for someone who'd been shouting. For about ten seconds I see Rudolf in half darkness before he dodges into his house. Now you ask me to recognize the pattern of his coat. And you're *paid* for what you do."

Beef remained calm.

"Not the pattern," he said, "the colour. Was this about the colour of the coat he was wearing?"

"So far as I remember."

"Had you ever met him before, going up to the house at night?"

"Can't say I had."

"So when he looked startled it might only have been because you saw him coming home at that time?"

"Pigs might fly. I should say he had something to be scared about."

Mrs. Dunton had been sitting looking downward to her clasped hands. Now Beef suddenly rounded on her and snapped out one of his brutally direct questions.

"When did you get back?" he asked.

He had not caught her unawares, however. She looked up with a face full of hostility and said: "I don't know what you mean."

"Oh, yes, you do. You left here some months ago when you got the sack from the house. How long have you been back here?"

"Who says I am back here?" asked Mrs. Dunton. "Who says I'm not just visiting?"

"And what the hell's it got to do with you?" Dunton shouted.

"Everything about everyone on this estate has got to do with me because—in case you happen to forget it—I'm trying to find out who killed Cosmo Ducrow. If you won't tell me when you got back I'll tell you. It was on the night of the murder."

"If you know so bloody much," said Dunton, "what you want to ask questions for?"

"To give you a chance to show you're afraid to answer. Now Mrs. Dunton, what time did you get back that night?"

"I don't know. 'Leven o'clock, I daresay."

"Did you go out again?"

"No."

"You sat here talking?"

Dunton broke in.

"Of course we sat talking. What do you expect? She'd come back, hadn't she, after being away? We had things to talk about."

"And you were still talking when Mr. Gray phoned at four o'clock in the morning?"

"You know everything, don't you?"

"So you only had to put a coat on and go out. You would have seen if anyone else had come down the drive after the shouts were heard and before Rudolf Ducrow showed up?"

"I never heard any shouts."

"But you were out there for five minutes or more before you saw Rudolf. Did you see anyone else in that time?"

"What do you think these gates are? A Zebra crossing? I saw nothing till Rudolf appeared."

"And heard nothing?"

"No."

"Did you see Mrs. Rudolf Ducrow that night?"

"Her? No."

"You didn't go up to the house?"

"Oh, for God's sake, haven't I told you we were both here talking?"

Beef turned to Dunton's wife again.

"You were dismissed from Mr. Ducrow's service, I understand?"

"I'd of gone if I hadn't of been."

"What were you sacked for?"

"Because there's some interfering cows who think too much of themselves and can't mind their own business and go running with every bit of spite they can think of, while their husbands are no better."

"So the Gabriels reported you?"

Mrs. Dunton stood up and showed a face which reminded me that Mrs. Gabriel had called her "a proper she-devil".

"Reported me?" she screamed. "I'll give her reports where she won't like them. The two-faced, evil-minded cat! And they were no better for listening to her."

"You seem to have a grudge against the Ducrow family?"

"Well, wouldn't you have? Listening to lies from those two."

"I'm wondering how far you would carry such a grudge."

"If you mean did she do the old man in the answer is 'no'," said Dunton. "Now, is there anything else, anything sensible, you want to ask before you go?"

Beef looked at him calmly.

"Yes," he said. "You seem to like to speak your mind about people. What do you think of Major Gulley?"

Dunton's sullen face seemed to grow animated, but certainly not with affection.

"Gulley? I'll tell you. He's a crook. A plain, dirty, swindling crook. He's been doing the old man for years and spending the money on all sorts of women. It was plain as a pikestaff but the old man and Gray trusted him. Nothing was too mean for him."

"That's a serious accusation," said Beef. "Have you got any proof of what you're saying?"

"Proof? That's a laugh. The old man himself had proof. They found out only about a week before he was killed. All of a sudden, for no reason, Mr. Ducrow sent for a chartered accountant, and he found that Gulley had been fiddling for years. Thousands of pounds involved."

"Why is he still here then?"

"It was all being gone into when Mr. Ducrow was murdered. The accountant had all the books. They say Gulley will do time for it."

"Who is 'they'?"

"Common talk."

"Yes, but whose? You're not on speaking terms with the Gabriels."

"Certainly not. It was Mills told me. I'd suspected it for a long time, though."

"Do you think Mills might be prejudiced?"

"Well, he does want to get married, and hoped to have that cottage Gulley is going to have. But I don't think it's that."

"Do the police know this?"

"Shouldn't think so. Mrs. Ducrow has too much to keep quiet herself to go talking about anyone else, and Gray would probably want to let him off."

"One last thing. Did you hear a car come in or out that night?"

"Funny thing—I did think in the morning I'd heard a car after we'd gone to bed, but I wasn't sure. I was tired when I did get in and so was the missis. I said in the morning I thought I'd heard something but she said she hadn't so I said no more about it."

Beef closed his notebook.

"That's all then."

Dunton stood up.

"I wouldn't have your job for anything," he said. "Nasty, dirty business it must be, prying into other people's lives. Still, I daresay you like it."

Beef looked at him steadily.

"No," he said, "I don't like it. There are even times when I hate it. Good night to you."

He marched out of the lodge while I rather uncomfortably followed him.

In the cold darkness we walked side by side towards the house. Beef halted for a moment at the bend of the drive near the little pavilion and looked in the direction of the place where the body had been found.

"I've a good mind to throw this case up," he announced.

Though on the previous evening I had suggested this I felt now that it had grown more interesting. There seemed to be so many issues and possibilities.

"Dunton was more than half right," he went on. "This detection can be a dirty business. Poking about in other people's affairs and getting them to commit themselves."

"You mean that you're sorry for the murderer?"

"I don't say that. But I do get sick of it all sometimes. Digging out little secrets. Causing unhappiness, very likely, to people who have done no harm."

"Aren't you being rather morbid? After all, you're seeing that an innocent man isn't punished, aren't you?"

"There aren't any innocent men," said Beef gloomily.

"Innocent of murder, I mean. Unless you agree with Oscar Wilde that we're all murderers of one kind or another. 'For each man kills the thing he loves'."

"I don't go much on poetry, but I understand what you mean. And there's one thing about this case that's as plain as a pikestaff. There's more ways of killing a dog than choking it to death with butter. There's more people concerned in the killing of Cosmo Ducrow than the one who bashed his head in."

"You mean there was a conspiracy?"

"Not necessarily. Some of those who played their part may not have known what they were doing. I tell you, Townsend, this is a very ugly business."

"I warned you yesterday…"

"I don't mean that. It's not the danger I'm worried about."

"You admit there is danger then?"

"Not yet. But there may be later."

"For you and me?"

I could hear a small, irritating chuckle in Beef's voice.

"You don't need to get windy. Keep your eyes open and your door locked and you'll be all right. They won't think *you* know too much."

"And you?"

"I can look after myself," said Beef.

We were approaching the front door so I said no more. But I had a strong presentiment of evil as we came into the silent hall. It was as though we were being watched by someone who was asking how much we knew, how dangerous we were, how we could be silenced.

10

B eef put the gun in the cloakroom but kept Rudolf's jacket over his arm as he entered the library. I watched narrowly the three people who were again awaiting us there and saw their eyes go straight to the jacket. Unfortunately Beef did not give me time to study their reactions for he held up the garment like a trophy and asked if any of them had seen it before.

"It looks like an old jacket of Rudolf's," said Mrs. Ducrow.

"When did you see it last?"

"I've no idea. He wore it once or twice last summer, I think."

"You, Major Gulley?"

The Major's ebullient manner had quietened considerably, I noticed.

"Can't say at all."

"Mr. Gray?"

"I seem to have seen it lying about somewhere of late. Was it in this house, I wonder?"

"I have reason to believe," said Beef in his witness-box voice, "that this jacket was worn on the night of the 12th." He named the night of the murder. His pompous phraseology seemed to irritate everyone. "I notice that attempts have recently been made to clean it, and I deduce from these that there may have been bloodstains on it. I am sending it for expert examination. If any blood has been on it I am quite sure that traces of it will be found."

"Where did you find it?" asked Gray.

"In the cloakroom of Rudolf Ducrow's house."

"What do you intend to do if there are traces of blood in the cloth?"

"There's only one thing I could do. I should have to hand it over to the police."

"Wouldn't that be to strengthen the case against Rudolf?"

"It might be. But I warned you when I undertook this case, Mr. Gray, that I should look for the truth and withhold no material information from the police."

Mrs. Ducrow began to speak loudly and vehemently.

"You see what he's doing, Theo? He is trying to make Rudy guilty. He's like the rest of them!"

Gray was calmer but he, too, seemed somewhat perturbed.

"It's perfectly true that we want you to find the truth," he said, "and we are satisfied that when it is found it will clear Rudolf Ducrow. But surely you must see that he is already in danger of being arrested, and if you produce another piece of evidence which points to him he may be sent for trial before we can save him?"

Beef answered thoughtfully.

"I don't think there is any danger of an innocent man being hanged for the murder of Cosmo Ducrow," he said.

Mrs. Ducrow was hysterical now.

"Get rid of him!" she cried. "I thought I could trust him. You must get rid of him, Theo, before he does any more harm. If Rudy is made to suffer I shall kill myself!"

Beef and Gray both looked at her as though in wonder.

"You should not talk like that," said Beef inadequately.

"All the same," said Gray quietly, "don't you think it might be as well if you did give up this case? We would, of course, cover all your fees and compensate you for any loss you may suffer."

"No," said Beef obstinately. "I can't pack in now. I've gone too far already. But I will promise you that no innocent person shall suffer. Now there's one or two things I want to ask Major Gulley."

"But he was not here that night," said Gray.

"I've already given you a very full account of my movements." Gulley sounded aggrieved. "I've told you they can be checked with the porter at the flats. If you're going to demand the name of the lady who was with me you're wasting your time."

"No. It's not that." I felt sick with apprehension, guessing what was to come.

"I can't think what else..."

"What's this about you cooking the books?" asked Beef.

It was clear that all three of them had feared some such question as this and that they were stunned by it. The first to recover himself was Gray.

"You are making a very ill-timed and unjust reference to something which is of no possible concern to you," he said. "Major Gulley has now our complete confidence. Nothing in his conduct of Mr. Ducrow's affairs has any connection whatever with the murder."

"You don't deny..." began Beef.

"I neither deny nor admit anything, Sir." Gray spoke with dignity. "There is no need for me to do so. You have been listening to gossip which grossly distorts the facts. Mrs. Ducrow and I are perfectly satisfied with Major Gulley's work for the estate."

"Was Mr. Ducrow?"

"Mr. Ducrow is dead. We do not wish to speculate on what opinions he may have held. Now, are you prepared to withdraw from this investigation?"

"No."

"Then I must cancel your authority to make enquiries on our behalf and instruct you to leave the house tomorrow."

"Just as you like about that."

Gulley nervously cleared his throat.

"Aren't we being a little hasty?" he said. "If Beef withdraws he will have to give all the information he has acquired..."

"I see what you mean. We'll discuss this tomorrow."

Beef elected to have what he called "a game of darts at the local" that evening and left me to face a most uncomfortable evening with our hosts. We all carefully avoided any reference to the subject which was on our minds, and I did my best to make general conversation without even mentioning Beef. I recalled my schooldays at St. Lawrence College, Ramsgate, and gave them some vignettes of my life as an insurance agent and later inspector. Then I turned to literature and drew what I thought were some rather clever comparisons between writers whose names, I consider, confer a certain kudos on those who can discuss their work intelligently—such modern giants as Christopher Isherwood and Christopher Fry, Edith Sitwell and Elizabeth Bowen, W. H. Auden and V. S. Pritchett, Stephen Spender and Louis MacNeice, a galaxy of illustrious names which I thought would arouse their interest. It was not long, however, before I saw that I was wasting my energy, for Gray confessed to a taste for such old-fashioned and bourgeois novelists as Conrad and Galsworthy, while Gulley could talk of nothing but "Westerns". As soon as I could politely do so I took my leave and went up to bed.

Alone in my room I wished heartily that Beef had not left the house tonight. I felt curiously nervous, and although my door was locked I did not like the thought of undressing and lying unprotected in bed. Footsteps passed in the corridor several times and once paused for a full minute outside my door. I forced my breathing to be audible as a very light regular snoring sound which I hoped would seem natural to the listener on the threshold.

But I could not sleep. Even when there was silence in the house about me, suggesting that all were at last asleep, I found myself tossing and turning and wide awake. I could see the window from where I lay and knew that some of the clouds of the afternoon had been driven away and there was a fairly clear starry sky, while the wind seemed to have dropped.

Somewhere in this house or in one of the lodges, I reflected, a murderer was as restless as I, knowing that he or she had committed a brutal crime for which society would show no forgiveness. But I knew better than to speculate on his or her identity.

Then suddenly something told me to look out of the window. Had I heard a sound or was the warning of a psychic nature? I shall never know, but it was urgent enough to make me jump out of bed and cross the room. I looked down by the fitful and uncertain starlight and was rewarded by seeing something which, Beef afterwards admitted, provided him with an important suggestion. Someone was coming round the corner of the house walking swiftly towards the drive. I leaned out to see who it was, but the person evidently did not mean to be recognized for over his head was an open umbrella. No rain was falling, so this could only be intended to conceal his identity from the windows above. I thought I saw a man's shoes, but could not be certain in that light.

What a diabolically clever disguise, I thought, for by holding the umbrella high above his head or down as low as possible he could conceal even his height. Who was this lonely being, I asked myself, leaving the house at half-past one in the morning? It could be anyone. Gabriel? Rudolf? Theo Gray? Mills? Major Gulley? Dunton? Even Beef? Or one of the women who had put on a man's shoes? Freda Ducrow? Mrs. Gabriel? Zena? Mrs. Dunton? There was nothing to suggest the identity unless the absentee could be discovered by a tour of inspection of the bedrooms. Beef was capable of this, I thought, and resolved therefore to keep the information till the morning.

I woke early, and finding that it was a freakishly fine day with sunlight breaking through and the air quite warm, I decided to go out for a stroll before breakfast. Perhaps I would find some trace of last night's mysterious noctambulist.

It was eight o'clock when I stepped out on the terrace and found that I was not the first up. Theo Gray had brought his newspaper out and was glancing at it as he strolled towards me.

"Wonderful morning," he said.

I wanted to walk round the house and not stop to talk so I said, "Yes, wonderful," rather curtly and pressed on. I had an uncomfortable feeling that he was smiling at me.

I could find no trace of any footprints, but soon Beef joined me and I told him what I had seen during the night.

"Oh, yes?" he said indifferently, once again seeking to belittle any help I might give to his investigations.

"Perhaps we might see some footprints."

He laughed rudely.

"You don't half have some old-fashioned ideas," he said. "And why on earth did you start making that noise like a sow in furrow when I was coming to your room last night? You shouldn't do that, you know, someone might hear you. I was just coming along to tell you that me'n my partner were unbeaten at darts last night."

"I'm sure I should have been most interested," I said sarcastically.

"So you might have been when I told you who my partner was."

"Who was it?"

"Mills, the chauffeur," said Beef.

"Perhaps it was also you who was walking about with an umbrella up last night?"

"No. I never use an umbrella."

"Well, I'm getting fed up with this case," I said. "You left me alone with those three all the evening."

"Didn't you learn anything?"

"We didn't discuss the case. Look here, Beef, are you really getting anywhere?"

"Slow but sure," said Beef.

"I'm not asking you to tell me, but have you any idea of who the murderer may be?"

"Have you?"

I thought for a moment, then admitted that I had not.

"Just if you were to guess?" cajoled Beef.

"Well, if I were to say at this point who I think is guilty, it would be nothing but guesswork. Sheer guesswork. So I'll do what the readers of detective novels do and choose the most unlikely."

"Go on, then," said Beef.

"I'll say either Mrs. Dunton or Theo Gray."

His face grew grave.

"Those seem to you the most unlikely?"

"Just about. Yes."

"Well, you're wrong."

"Both guesses?"

"Yes."

"I should like you to state that a little more definitely so that there can be no question afterwards of what you meant."

"Very well. I tell you absolutely definitely that neither Theo Gray nor Mrs. Dunton killed Cosmo Ducrow."

"Good enough. That narrows the field."

"I may be able to put one or two more out of the running in a day or two," said Beef.

"Process of elimination, eh? Well, I hope it doesn't take too long. I want to get back to London."

11

No indication was given at breakfast of whether or not Beef was to retain his authority to investigate, but after the meal was finished Gray called us aside.

"I have been thinking over this matter," he said, "and I've reached the conclusion that you would not be acting as you are unless you felt pretty certain that you can clear up the case against Rudolf. I don't ask you to give me any assurances about that. I simply remind you that it is the concern of everyone that he should not be tried for this murder."

"I understand what you mean," said Beef. "I'll go so far as to say that it may well be avoided, but I'm afraid he will be charged and brought before a magistrate. That is, if the jacket proves to have been bloodstained. If you'll continue to give me your co-operation, Mr. Gray, I believe I can get at the truth."

"Very well. But I hope you won't discover any more evidence which seems to be against Rudolf."

We were interrupted just then by the arrival of the young man in question, who came in breathless and eager to tell us some strange news.

"Extraordinary thing," he said. "My car was stolen last night."

"Stolen?"

"Yes. I left it outside my house as I always do. This morning it was gone."

Beef pulled out his notebook.

"Was it locked?" he asked.

"The doors, you mean? No. The ignition key was out, but that doesn't mean much, as you know. I've lost several of them since I had the car. One yesterday, as a matter of fact, through dropping it carelessly in one of my big overcoat pockets."

"Didn't you hear anything in the night?"

"No. But then I always leave the old bus at the top of the slope so that I can start it in the morning. All the thief had to do was to jump in, take off the handbrake and away. He could start the engine at the bottom of the slope a quarter of a mile from my house. I should never hear him."

It was evident from Beef's expression that whatever else he had or had not anticipated this was a development as unexpected to him as to the rest of us. But was it a development? Rudolf himself asked that very question.

"Think it has anything to do with the murder?"

I was amused to see that by this blunt enquiry Beef was hoist with his own petard.

"Hard to say. Very hard to say," he intoned and sucked his pencil stump. "Might have, and then again might not. You better report it to the police in any case. I shall be calling on Inspector Stute this morning and will mention it to him, but it should be reported in the ordinary way to the local police officer."

When we were alone I enjoyed a minor triumph over Beef.

"You see? What I saw in the night was not so unimport-
ant after all."

"What was that?"

I reminded him of the mysterious figure under the umbrella.

"It's clear," I said, "that some one from this house had an
interest in removing Rudolf's car last night. Perhaps he wished
to immobilize him."

Beef said nothing, and when I offered to drive him to see
Inspector Stute he replied sulkily that he would just as soon
walk. In the circumstances and because it was such a lovely
morning for November I agreed with him and we set out,
Beef carrying a brown-paper parcel.

When we came to the little pavilion Beef elected to look
around it again. I was sure that he was doing this with the
sole purpose of annoying me because I was anxious to get
over our interview with Stute. I could see a little smile on
his face and knew it of old.

"Oh, come on, Beef," I said. "Don't let's waste any more
time."

He seemed to be looking for something which would justify
the delay, and was relieved to see an old overcoat and hat
hanging there. He began with painful deliberation to examine
these.

"More bloodstains?" I asked sarcastically.

"No," said Beef. "No bloodstains on this, I think."

He peered into the hat, a greasy and battered relic, then
hung it up again.

"I'm going on," I said angrily.

He thereupon began a silly piece of play-acting.

"Could we have been seen from the house?" he asked.
"Coming in here, I mean?"

I looked round.

"No. Of course not."

"Then we'll go back to the drive the same way. Don't cut across to the drive farther down." He assumed an absurd air of secrecy. "That is, if you value your life."

More childishness, I thought. But I followed his route to humour him.

I noticed several things before we reached the park gates, things which might have some bearing on the case, but with Beef in his present mood I decided to keep my observations to myself. I saw, for instance, that although until now there had been no sign of cattle grazing in the park, this morning there were some Jersey cows there. And I noticed that Dunton, though he pretended to be busy behind some rhododendron bushes, was watching us closely.

At the lodge gates we were assailed by two Boxer dogs and heard Mrs. Rudolf Ducrow shouting "Malik! Vishinsky!" from somewhere in the rear of the house, while the Duntons had evidently resolved against any further attempt at secrecy in the matter of Mrs. Dunton's return for she was vigorously shaking a mat at her front door.

As we approached the village Beef was hailed by a tubby little man lounging at a shop door. His dull red cheeks and slightly glazed eyes suggested to my trained observation that he was an habitual if not an excessive beer-drinker. He greeted Beef as "Sarge" and was in turn called "Fred", so that I guessed him to have been one of the locals with whom Beef had been hobnobbing and playing darts on the previous evening. And when we reached a house with a notice COUNTY POLICE on it, I was not surprised to find that the local sergeant was already an acquaintance of his.

"Lovely morning," said this character rubbing his hands.

"Lovely," agreed Beef. "This is Mr. Townsend, who writes my cases up for me," he added in his grand manner.

"Wish I had someone to do that for me," said Sergeant Eels as he shook hands with me. "This young constable I've got is too busy making reports on his own."

Sergeant Eels was a thickset vigorous-looking man whose sharp waxed moustache jumped about on his lip when he talked as though it had a life of its own. He had a loud voice and cheerful manner.

"Rudolf Ducrow will be down presently," said Beef. "His car's been pinched in the night."

"Not surprised," said Eels. "He leaves it outside his house every night, right at the top of the slope. You want to see Inspector Stute, I suppose? You'll find him along at the Buck and Arrow, where he's staying. But have a cup of char before you go. It's just being made." He raised his voice to be heard by the constable whom I had seen through the door to an inner room. "Spender-Hennessy! Is that char ready?"

"Coming up, Sarge."

"Decent young bloke," said Eels. "But a bit too keen, if you know what I mean. Well, he's not finished his training long and you know what they are when they're young. I tell him to please himself. 'If you want to be up at all hours you can', I say, 'I like my sleep.' Still, he's had one or two nice little cases, if he has got a rather cheeky way of talking."

"*What* did you say his name was?"

"Spender-Hennessy."

"I don't know what's happening to the Force, upon my soul, I don't. Where do names like that come from, I should like to know?"

"Straight out of the *New Statesman*," I put in drily, but nobody took any notice, of course.

The young constable appeared carrying two mugs, then went back for two more. Soon the room resounded to that curious mixture of gurgling and suction which suggests that policemen are enjoying hot tea.

"So you like a bit of a look-round at night, do you?" said Beef expansively to Constable Spender-Hennessy. "I was the same myself at one time. Couldn't keep me off my bicycle after dark when I was a beginner, same as you."

"Really?" said the young man in a bored voice. "You were in the Police Force, were you?"

"This is Sergeant Beef," said Eels with shocked emphasis. "*The* Sergeant Beef. And this is Mr. Townsend, who works with him."

"I'm afraid I don't go to the pictures much. What is it? Cross-talk comedy?"

"You'll get cross-talk if you're not careful, young man." Eels turned to Beef. "It's only his inexperience," he said apologetically. "They fill 'em up with so much theory nowadays they think it's all in books and microscopes."

"I know," said Beef. He seemed to be in no way put out, and smiled to the constable. "I was going to ask you if you happened to be cycling anywhere near Hokestones on the night of the murder?"

"Not actually," the young man said.

"What on earth do you mean by that?" asked Beef. "Were you or weren't you?"

Constable Spender-Hennessy smiled loftily.

"I was and I wasn't," he said. "I did not go so far as the lodge gates, but I had a gander up the road towards them."

"See anything out of the ordinary?"

"Definitely."

Beef turned to Eels.

"Does he mean he did or he didn't?"

"I think he means he did, don't you?"

"Definitely. I saw Mrs. Dunton walking up the road."

"That was round about eleven?"

"Eleven seven."

"I suppose you've told Inspector Stute that?"

Constable Spender-Hennessy gave a bored sigh.

"Do you suppose I might have failed to do so? I need scarcely say I was able to give him all the details he required." He turned to me. "Do you really make a living out of books about this character? I should have thought he was too corny even for detective novels."

I was secretly a little pleased.

"Of course, I have to do a good deal of manipulation," I said. "Bring out the nuances. Touch up the *dénouement*. Make him *comme il faut*."

"Give him *esprit de corps*?" suggested the constable. "And *je ne sais quoi*, perhaps?"

I saw that he was attempting to be funny at my expense, and spoke briskly to Beef. "Isn't it time we went to see Inspector Stute?"

"No hurry," said Beef maddeningly. "I haven't finished my tea yet." He turned again to Constable Spender-Hennessy. "So you were able to give the Inspector all the details he required, were you? Well, that's very nice, I'm sure. And what else did you see that night?"

"Nothing, actually."

"You didn't notice what lights were on in the two lodges?"

"I can see no reason why I should have. If I had been aware that a murder was proceeding I should doubtless have taken note of a number of things. Unfortunately we are not asked to the preview in a case of that sort."

"So you had nothing else to tell Inspector Stute?"

"Absolutely nothing."

"What time did you go to bed that morning?"

"In the region of six."

"And where were you between five and six?"

"Does it matter? After all, the murder took place hours earlier than that."

"I would just like to know."

"I was on the London road most of the time."

"See any cars coming towards the village?"

"Yes. Why?"

"What did you see?"

I felt it was a minor triumph for Beef when at this point Constable Spender-Hennessy produced a green morocco-bound notebook stamped in gold with the letters G.S.-H. He flicked back some pages.

"At about five-five," he said, "an old Lagonda car, number EYN 985, was driven rather fast down the lane which runs from the London road to Hawden. It seemed to go through the village."

"Towards Hokestones?"

"Could be," said the constable airily.

"Anything more?"

"Yes. About eight or ten minutes later the same car, driven much faster now, returned. I saw it take the bend and disappear towards London."

"Could you see how many were in it?"

"Certainly not. It had blinding headlights."

"And you didn't think that worth mentioning to the Inspector?"

"Actually, no. It happened several hours after the murder. I can't see what possible connection it can have."

"Oh, you can't? Then let me tell you, young man, that you ought to have your head seen to."

"Really!"

"Yes, really. Actually. Definitely. Absolutely. The car that passed you went up the drive at Hokestones and back."

"How can you possibly know that?"

"It was at the scene of the crime for several minutes. That car belongs to Major Gulley."

"Interesting, but not conclusive," said Constable Spender-Hennessy coolly.

"Oh, go and take a running jump at yourself," said Beef, voicing a sentiment in which we all most heartily joined.

12

Chief Inspector Stute of the Special Branch is a man for whom I have the highest regard. He had been in charge of the investigation of several previous cases in which Beef had blundered on a solution, and although I suspected that he attributed most of Beef's success to luck he was fairly tolerant of my old ex-policeman. Perhaps he realized, too, that Beef so much belonged to the world of such people as the Gabriels, Mills and Dunton that he often learned facts from them which they would not willingly reveal to the police. At all events, he usually listened to Beef and sometimes gave him information in return for the scraps of tittle-tattle which Beef retailed.

The Buck and Arrow turned out to be a Tudor inn which had been taken over by one of the hotel catering combines. It had an impressive sign painted by a commercial artist of some talent and swinging in a wrought-iron frame. It had diamond-paned windows in great profusion and a wealth—no, a positive El Dorado—of oak beams. It also had a receptionist's office near the front door. We approached the young lady in this.

"Chief Inspector Stute?" she said. "Eh'm effreyed he's engaged at the moment."

"That's all right," said Beef looking a little uncomfortable, "I'll wait till he comes out."

"Eh'm effreyed he has someone with him."

"What, old Stute? You can't..."

"The gentleman is in conference."

"Tell him Sergeant Beef's got some vital information for him, will you?"

"Eh'm effreyed..."

He turned to me in exasperation.

"Here, Townsend, you talk to her. She's more your sort than mine. Find out where he is, for goodness' sake. We're wasting half the morning."

I came forward and raised my hat. After a few minutes I managed to discover that Stute was upstairs in the "Residents' Drawing-Room" with "two other gentlemen" and had asked not to be disturbed.

"That's all right," said Beef. "He won't mind me." And before the young lady could say any more, or repeat herself, he had bolted for the stairs.

There was an angry "Oh, come in!" in answer to Beef's tap and certainly no pleasure shown in the three faces turned towards us.

"Well? Oh, it's you. I might have known," was Chief Inspector Stute's welcome.

He looked a little, but not much, older than I remembered him on previous occasions. His thick grey hair was more silvery but just as thick and carefully combed, his neat military moustache as clipped and his clothes as well pressed. His appearance contrasted with the ready made serge suit and stringy tie which Beef wore. And Beef's manner, in the presence of a man so distinguished in his old service, became rather awed, I noticed.

"You'll excuse me, Chief Inspector," he said, "but I've got a little information in the Ducrow case which I think you ought to have."

Stute exchanged glances with the other two, and I guessed that Beef had mentioned the very subject of their discussion.

"Oh, you have? I suppose you've come to tell me that Rudolf was Freda's lover? Or that a car was near the corpse in the early morning? Or that Zena Ducrow was up at the house that night?"

Beef's mouth opened like that of a fish on a slab.

"I..." he began.

"Or is it that Mrs. Dunton returned to her husband's house that evening?" went on Stute, enjoying Beef's humiliation. "Or that they were still up when Gray phoned?"

Beef was never very good at taking a joke against himself, and now lost his temper.

"No!" he shouted. "I've come to bring you this!"

He threw the brown-paper parcel which he had been hugging all the morning on the table among them. Without troubling to unwrap it Stute continued to talk calmly.

"One of Rudolf's jackets, I suppose, which you think he wore on the night of the murder."

"One of Rudolf's jackets," said Beef, "which I think has had bloodstains cleaned from it."

Stute smiled.

"All right, Beef. I'm not saying you don't do some good work sometimes. I was pulling your leg just now. These two gentlemen are Forster and Liphook of the Special Branch. This old warhorse is Sergeant Beef, who gets himself employed as a private investigator and is less of a fool than he looks." I found that I was being omitted and coughed. "Oh, and this is Townsend," added Stute. "So you've found the coat he wore? Where was it?"

"Hanging in Rudolf's cloakroom."

"We searched there."

"Then either you didn't think it was of interest, or it was not there then. I might not have noticed it if I had not heard from Mrs. Gabriel that such a jacket of Rudolf's had been hanging on a peg at Hokestones till the night of the 12th."

"What else can you tell us?"

Beef quite honestly gave them the results of his enquiries, keeping nothing back, but drawing no inferences either. The unlocked french windows in the library, Mrs. Ducrow's intemperate habits, Mrs. Gabriel's apparently unreasonable suspicion of Mrs. Dunton, the various footsteps heard by Mrs. Gabriel, the certainty that it was Gulley's old Lagonda which had been driven up to the scene of the crime, the missing croquet mallet, the back door which was open ajar when Rudolf was coming through the kitchen that night, the reason for Zena's visit to Cosmo and his reaction to the information she brought, the suspicion that Gulley had been swindling Cosmo and that he knew it; even, though rather grudgingly, the figure under the umbrella which I had observed last night and the discovery this morning that Rudolf's car had been stolen—all this was gone over by Beef in straightforward and businesslike terms. Stute said little, made a jotting or two and finally thanked the Sergeant.

"Some useful stuff there," he said, "but it does not alter our main conclusion, which is probably the same as yours. Either Rudolf is a pretty stupid sort of murderer, or else it is all an elaborate plant to try to make him look guilty."

Beef nodded.

"Take the croquet mallet," said Stute. "If Rudolf did it, why should he choose the very mallet he always used? Wasn't that asking for trouble?"

The man called Liphook spoke slowly.

"You know what I think about that," he said. "Rudolf might easily have been clever enough to use it on the grounds that it would remove suspicion from him rather than otherwise for the very reason you've just given. He may have done everything so obviously that it looks like a plant."

"That's ingenious," I couldn't help saying.

"Quite possible, too. It would account for this coat. Did he invite you to the cloakroom where it was hanging, Beef?"

"Yes."

"There you are. But what is interesting about the croquet mallet is that only his fingerprints appeared on it and there was no sign of smudging as there would have been if someone had used gloves."

"What condition was it in when it was found?"

"Oh, it had been used for the murder all right. One flat end of the hammer part was a mass of blood."

"What about the missing mallet?"

"Difficult to understand," admitted Stute. "Who noticed it? Gulley? Everything from that fellow's pretty suspect. It might be a red herring. It might have some quite ordinary explanation."

"I should be grateful for one or two technical points," said Beef. "The doctor's report, for instance."

"I haven't it here," said Stute, "but it was very much what you'd expect. 'Cause of Death' sounds rather inadequate for those mallet blows—the poor wretch had practically no skull left. It was a most shocking crime from that point of view— quite unnecessary violence. Yet not with any idea of concealing identity, for all the blows were on the back of the head, none on the face."

"What about time of death?" asked Beef.

"Very difficult to gauge. The doctor did not examine the corpse until half-past nine on the following morning. He'll only say that he thinks it was after twelve-thirty and before five-thirty. Gives a nice wide range, doesn't it?"

"Yes."

There was a long silence. Then Beef asked if any of the people connected with the case had criminal records.

"Funny you should ask that," said Stute, "because there are two—both old ones. Gulley did six months for some cheque frauds on hotels when he was a man of twenty-seven. Mills was a Borstal boy: burglary at sixteen. Gone straight since then. Strange that old Ducrow should have had two men with records working for him. I don't think he or anyone else knew of them though."

"Perhaps not," said Beef.

"Well, we come back to Rudolf. Plant or not, we could get him hanged on the evidence we now have, and if the jacket turns out to have had bloodstains cleaned from it I don't see that we can do anything but arrest him."

"Nor do I," said Beef. "As a matter of fact I shouldn't be sorry to see you do so."

That seemed to me like treachery to his employers, but I said nothing.

"Why?" demanded Stute.

"Because as you say there are only two possibilities. Either he is a murderer, in which case he may as well be tried as soon as possible. Or else he is the victim of an elaborate plant, in which case he's in danger."

"Do you really think so?"

"Well, if someone killed Cosmo and tried to pin it on Rudolf, that someone must be getting very worried that Rudolf is not arrested. Sooner or later that someone is going to take the matter into his or her hands."

"I see what you mean."

"One or two other things. Which Borstal Institution was Mills in?"

"Roffington."

"Good. And have you traced the woman whom Gulley took back to the flat in Montrevor House that night?"

"Yes. Her name is Esmeralda Tobyn, and she lives at 18 Peckham Avenue, Putney Common."

"Have you any details of Rudolf's army service?"

"Yes. He did very well. Had a breakdown in 1945, though, and was sent to an Army mental hospital for a few weeks. Discharged as fit. Nothing unusual about that, as you know."

"No. Well I'm very much obliged to you, Chief Inspector, for the information you have given me. Very much obliged."

"I suppose now you'll go away and come back with some wonderful new theory unrelated to either of our alternatives?"

"Just now I don't see any theory that accounts for everything."

"If it's a plant," said Liphook, "it should be easy to discover who is guilty because a scheme as elaborate as that must have taken weeks to work out."

"If that were the case," said Beef heavily, "I shouldn't think it was a plant because whatever else is uncertain about this business I'm pretty sure that there was no scheming beforehand. It all happened that night like spontaneous combustion."

"Then Rudolf's guilty?" smiled Liphook.

"I am not giving any opinion yet," announced Beef.

I could see that the three experts were rather amused at the old boy though I think they were glad of his bits and pieces of information.

"Are you going to stay up at the house?" asked Stute. "It's not my idea of a cosy home from home."

"I think it would be an excellent idea if we moved here," I said.

"What, with all this old oak? Not me. I like a pub to be a pub, not an antique shop. Besides, that piece downstairs with the plum in her mouth would drive me crackers. We've got to see what goes on up there."

"You watch out for yourself," said Stute quite seriously.

Beef grinned.

"I will," he said.

13

All next day we were waiting for the expert's report on Rudolf's jacket. I gathered that if there had been any bloodstains, however well the cloth had been cleaned traces would remain.

At the house, in which Beef insisted on staying, there was a tense and trying atmosphere. Theo Gray would scarcely speak to us; Freda Ducrow spent most of the time in her room and, I suspected, was drinking heavily. Major Gulley put up a show of defiance. Even Gabriel seemed to have lost his faith in Beef—perhaps, I thought, because the latter had given gratuitous information to the police. It was a sullen household and one on tenterhooks.

Beef himself seemed at a loss, and for the first part of the morning sat in an easy chair, smoking his pipe and reading one of the more irresponsible daily newspapers. When I tackled him about this he said that there was nothing much he could do until the report on the jacket came through.

"I've done all my preliminary investigation," he said. "Now we must wait for something to turn up."

I tried to make him see that this was not the right attitude for him to take, and asked whether he thought any of the better-known detectives whom he sought to emulate would be content to sit in an armchair reading while a murderer remained at large, to which he replied characteristically that it all depended. I was about to retort sarcastically when Gabriel came in and said rather sulkily that Mills wanted to speak to Beef alone.

I had never liked that young man, whose shifty eyes and reserved manner contrasted, I thought, with the open *bonhomie* of Rudolf Ducrow. But when Beef stood up and prepared to go out to the garage I decided to accompany him.

"He said 'alone'," Beef pointed out.

I made a derisory noise such as old-fashioned writers used to interpret as "Pshaw!" and kept close behind Beef. Mills was waiting in the yard.

"Come up to my room," he said in his secretive way. Then, seeing that I intended to follow, he asked: "What about him?"

"He's harmless, Bomb," said Beef.

I was not surprised to find that they were on terms which allowed them to use nicknames to one another, for Beef has, I admit, a gift for familiarity with such people and I had known him just as matey with a man whom he afterwards caused to be charged with murder. Nor did I mind being called "harmless", if it was in a good cause.

We found the room over the garage which Mills occupied a cosy place with two wicker armchairs and an electric fire. A photo of a flashy-looking girl was on the table and an array of bottles—shaving-lotion, brilliantine, eau-de-Cologne and so on—which would have been better suited, I thought, to a lady's apartment.

"Sit down, Sarge. I've got something to tell you. I didn't mean to let this out because I thought it might come in useful."

"What d'you mean by 'useful'?"

Mills looked uncomfortable.

"Well, you know. Might be worth something to someone."

"So that's it, is it? Well, let me tell you this, young Bomb. You can get into serious trouble for withholding information in an affair of this kind. I don't say that if your information is any good I won't make you a little present when the case is over, but don't imagine you've got anything to sell, because you haven't."

"O.K., Sarge. Don't get worked up. I said I was going to tell you."

Mills lit a cigarette from the stump of the one he had just finished.

"I saw something that night. The night of the murder, I mean."

"What time?"

"That's where you've got me. I never thought to look. It was some time in the small hours, I think, because I'd been asleep for a long time. I don't know for certain what woke me up, as a matter of fact. I think it was the yard door slamming to."

He led us to the window.

"See that door there? It leads to the kitchen garden. Anyone coming to this yard from the terrace would use it. But when there's a bit of wind, as there was that night, it blows shut unless you're careful. It must have been the noise of it which woke me up. I went straight to the window."

Mills seemed to be playing for effect. He paused to take several pulls at his cigarette.

"Someone was crossing the yard," he said.

"Man or woman?"

"Don't know. All I could see was an open umbrella."

I jumped up with excitement.

"There you are!" I exclaimed. "I told you that what I saw the other night was important..."

Mills gave me a hard, narrow look.

"What did you see?" he asked, and I did not like the tone of his voice.

"Never mind Townsend," said Beef rudely. "He's always seeing something. Go on with what you were saying."

Mills continued to look at me, and if ever the word "murderous" was an apt one for a man's expression it was now.

"Go on, Bomb," said Beef gently.

Mills seemed to pull himself together.

"Whoever it was had put up an umbrella, though it wasn't raining and there was enough wind to make it rather difficult to hold. Seems they thought they might be seen from a window and didn't mean to be recognized."

"Call him 'he' for convenience," said Beef. "Where did he go?"

"Across to the furnace room. The door along to the left there—you can only just see it from here. He must have stepped in first then put down his umbrella because I couldn't see him even when he went in. I was just making up my mind to pull some clothes on and go down to see what it was all about when the umbrella was stuck out again, unfolded, and away he went under it, through the same door to the kitchen garden."

"So you went back to bed?"

An ugly cunning look came to the young man's face.

"No. I guessed what he had gone there for—could only have been one thing. He wanted to burn something. 'Gulley!' I thought. 'Gulley destroying some evidence of his swindling!' I'd forgotten for the minute that Gulley was supposed to be in London. So I pulled on some clothes and went down to look in the furnace."

"Were you in time?"

"No. At least—there were no papers or anything burning. But right on top of the coke there was something that I took to be a log of wood. A very smooth, round log though. I thought there must be a madman about the place—bringing a log to the furnace in the small hours of the morning. It wasn't until I got back to my room that I realized what it was: the heavy part of a croquet mallet. If there had been a pair of tongs handy I would have pulled it out, I daresay. But there wasn't. In the morning it had burnt right away."

"Is that all?"

"Isn't it enough? Doesn't it solve the whole thing for you."

"Not quite. There's still the little matter of identity, isn't there? However, I'm grateful to you, Bomb. I want you to promise me something very particular."

"What's that?"

"Not to tell anyone what you've told us. Anyone at all."

"Want all the credit for yourself, I suppose?"

"It's not that. Will you promise?"

"All right. I won't tell anyone."

"Thanks, Bomb. See you on the dartboard tonight?"

"You bet. We'll see those two again."

"Till tonight then."

We left the yard by the gate which, as Mills had indicated, led into the kitchen garden. As we opened it we almost walked into Dunton, who was leaning over a bed of culinary herbs.

He nodded, but in a rather unfriendly way, I thought. We were certainly out of favour that day.

"I want you to drive me over to Roffington this afternoon," said Beef.

I knew his trick of taking little excursions at my expense pretending that they were necessary to his enquiries when in fact all he wanted was an outing.

"What for?" I asked suspiciously.

"To see a friend of mine. Man called Piper."

"And what has a man called Piper to do with the Ducrow case?" I asked.

"You'll see."

The brief show of fine weather which we had enjoyed on the previous day was over and our drive was on wet and slippery roads and through heavy rain. I did not talk much for I had to concentrate on my driving to avoid skids. Beef, too, was silent. When I remarked on this he said that he was thinking, and I let it go at that.

We came at last to the rather dreary town of Roffington, and when Beef had consulted his notebook we drove to what must have been its ugliest street. All the houses were identical and hideously built of yellow bricks. We drew up at the one Beef indicated and knocked on a shabby front door.

After we had waited some minutes an untidy woman opened it.

"Mr. Piper in?" asked Beef.

"Well, he's not up yet. He was on night duty last night," she said resentfully. "I was just having ten minutes myself. Who shall I say?"

"Tell him Sergeant Beef is here."

A faint animation came to her face.

"Oh, yes, he's talked about you. Joined the police force together, didn't you? He didn't stay long at that, thank goodness. I told him I wouldn't be a policeman's wife for anything, and he give it up and took this job where he's been ever since. I'll tell him you're here. Better come through to the kitchen. I've been doing my ironing, but you can find somewhere to sit down. There's no fire in the front room."

We did find somewhere to sit down, but it was with difficulty. It was like sitting in the sorting-room of a laundry.

"You can see what *she* is," Beef whispered when she had left us. "Three weeks' washing here. She doesn't move till she has to. But he's all right."

After some minutes a heavily built humorous-looking man lumbered in and there were noisy greetings between him and Beef. Mr. Piper, it appeared, was known as "Old Windpipe", while Sergeant Beef had shrunk to a monosyllabic "Bill". They banged each other's backs, and said it was donkey's years, assured one another that they hadn't changed and seemed about to begin exchanging reminiscences when I interrupted.

"Wasn't there something you wanted to ask Mr. Piper?" I said.

Beef gave me an irate look but came to the point.

"Oh yes, there was one little thing. You've worked at the Borstal institution for twenty-odd years now, haven't you?"

"Twenty-three."

"So you must have had thousands through your hands. But I want you to try to remember one particular lad. Mills. Alan Geoffrey Mills. With you about twelve years ago at the age of sixteen for burglary."

"Remember him perfectly," said Mr. Piper at once, seeming to find this a matter of course. "In fact, you'd be surprised how many I do remember by name."

"Tell us about him," said Beef. "This is, of course, between ourselves."

"I better say at once I didn't like him," said Mr. Piper. "His conduct was always exemplary—at least, in official reports, which is what matters. He was never caught doing anything wrong all the time he was here, which didn't seem natural to me. I suspected that there were others taking the rap for him. Mind you, I've only got my private suspicions about that, with nothing to back them up. But I had a feeling that he was deep. Capable of scheming things out to put someone else in the wrong."

"Ah!" said Beef expressively.

"And I didn't like the affair he came in for, either. It read to me as though he'd given his mates away. I daresay I was prejudiced. If you were to see an official report about him it would tell another story. But he struck me as the kind of fellow who would scheme and plot to get someone else in trouble."

"Thanks, Windy. You've been very helpful. See, I'm investigating the Ducrow Case."

"Oh! Is Mills mixed up in that?"

"He's the chauffeur."

Mr. Piper whistled.

"I see why you ask. Well, I don't need to tell you that what I've said is between ourselves."

"No. You don't need to tell me," said Beef and gave his old friend a reassuring smile.

14

Next morning Beef was called to the telephone, and when he returned to the room in which I was sitting with Theo Gray and Mrs. Ducrow his face was grave.

"The report on Rudolf's jacket is through," he said. "Traces of human blood have been found."

Freda Ducrow began to cry quietly.

"Does that mean Rudy will be arrested?"

"I don't know," said Beef. "The Chief Inspector will do as he thinks proper, and certainly would not inform me of his plans."

"It's so dreadful," sobbed Freda. "Losing Cosmo, and now this. They couldn't find Rudy guilty, could they Theo?"

"No, no, my dear. How could they? We know Rudolf is incapable of it."

"But it looks so black against him."

"Perhaps that's in his favour," I said brightly. "Perhaps it looks too black. Too black to be natural, I mean."

Beef and Gray exchanged glances, seeming to agree that this was a silly thing to say.

"Even if they do arrest him," Gray assured Freda, "they could not possibly find him guilty. Every scrap of the evidence is circumstantial."

"But he might be tried. Oh, it's so awful. All those dreadful newspaper headlines! They seem to be positively baying after him, like bloodhounds."

"After the murderer, not him."

"But they think he is the murderer. Everyone does. Even these two think so."

I spoke for both of us.

"In England a man is innocent till he's proved guilty."

"That's small comfort when you've done your best to make him look guilty. Theo, I think I should like to go and see Ernest Wickham. He was my father's solicitor and mine, and I believe he could advise me what to do."

"By all means, my dear Freda, if you think it will be any comfort to you. He is certainly a very shrewd man."

"Will you phone him and ask if he will see me today? As soon as possible? I could drive down to Folkover in time for lunch."

Theo Gray went out to the telephone.

I knew that Folkover was about thirty miles away, the great Kentish watering-place between Folkestone and Dover from which there was a cross-channel service to Dilogne. I seemed to remember reading or hearing that Freda was a Folkover girl who had nursed Cosmo while he had been in hospital there.

Theo Gray returned to say that Ernest Wickham would expect her at about five o'clock.

"I'm going up to London myself," Gray added. "I'm going to see Sir Mordaunt Tiptree. If Rudolf should need an advocate he is certainly the man. Besides, one of us should go and see Cosmo's lawyers."

"Oh, I'm glad, Theo. And perhaps they won't arrest Rudy after all."

"Perhaps not. But we'll take every precaution."

To my surprise Beef chipped in:

"Mr. Townsend and I have to go to London today," he said. "Perhaps you would not mind giving us a lift?"

I could see that Theo Gray thought this pushing.

"I am going up by train," he said coldly.

When we were alone I asked Beef why on earth he wanted to go to London at this point when the case was beginning to grow interesting.

"You've got a terrible memory," he said. "What about Miss Esmeralda Tobyn of 18 Peckham Avenue, Putney Common? Forgetting her, were you?"

"The woman Gulley was with that night, you mean? I can't see what she has to do with the case."

"Perhaps she's the flowers that bloom in the spring tra-la," said Beef with grotesque attempts at elephantine comedy. "All the same we've got to see her."

"Shall I drive you up, then?"

"No. If Gray is going by train we might as well accompany him. The eleven-four he said, didn't he? We'll be on that, too."

At least, I thought, we should get out of this gloomy house with its overpowering atmosphere of watchfulness and evil. I would have an opportunity to go round to my flat and attend to private affairs which were always woefully neglected while I was on a case with Beef. I went up to my room and had started to prepare for the journey when I realized that I had not shut the door and could hear what was being said by two people in the passage who evidently took it for granted that the upper part of the house would be empty at this time.

I detest the idea of eavesdropping, but detection is the better part of valour and I found myself standing quite still listening. The speakers were Freda Ducrow and Major Gulley.

"Theo has arranged for me to see him at five. I should like you to come down with me."

"I can't do that. Theo has particularly asked me to be here today. The accountant is coming."

If they had spoken in natural voices I might not have been impelled to listen. But this was whispering—furtive and hurried.

"Then would you come down later? I know I shall need a drink as soon as I come from Wickham's."

"I suppose I could do that."

"We'll meet at the Marina Palace at six o'clock, then. Or as soon as I can get there."

"I'll be there."

"Are those two really going away today?"

"I hope so."

"Have you noticed Townsend? He's afraid. I can see it. The man's in fear of his life."

"I'm not surprised," said Gulley grimly.

"See you at six, then."

"I think I had better tell Theo I'm meeting you. He likes to know what is going on."

"All right."

They moved away, but to my relief neither of them passed my door. I went along and reported the whole conversation to Beef.

"That's good," he said. "That's the best bit of news you've given me for a long time."

"I think we're most unwise to go to London," I told him. "The accountant is coming today and it's far more important that you should see him and get details of Gulley's defalcations than go chasing after his girl friend."

"I've no intention of chasing after anyone's girl friend," said Beef pompously. "I have to interview the lady."

Just then Gabriel came down the passage.

"Will you both be here this afternoon?" asked Beef.

"Not me. It's my day off. I shall get away at noon and stay away for the rest of the day, believe you me."

"On your own?"

"Yes. We can't get out together very well."

"Pity. We shall be back in the early evening."

"O.K., Sarge. I'll tell the wife. Going to London are you? I wonder you don't pack up this job, straight I do. It's hopeless. I suppose they'll arrest Rudolf at any minute?"

"I daresay."

"I almost wish they'd get it over. I've had enough of murder mystery to last me a lifetime."

At half-past ten I brought my car round to the front door in order to be in plenty of time to get Beef to the station for the eleven-four. I could see him in the hall talking to Gray and Gulley, so I joined them.

"May we give you a lift to the station?" suggested Beef. "It will save you having your car brought out."

Gray looked at my rather shabby old car but seemed to decide to be gracious.

"Thank you. That's very kind," he said smiling, then turning to Gulley he asked him to cancel his order to Mills.

The three of us climbed in and I began to drive to the station.

"Pity about these frauds of Gulley's," said Beef apropos of nothing.

"I should prefer that we did not discuss that matter," said Gray. "Mrs. Ducrow and Rudolf and I are, after all, the only people who are affected by anything Major Gulley may have done, and we have decided to follow a certain course in the matter."

"Very good of you all. I hope Major Gulley appreciates it. I understand he was to have had a cottage for himself?"

"Cosmo had decided that. I see no reason not to fulfil his wishes."

Gray looked straight ahead of him and Beef seemed, for once in his life, to feel snubbed. But when we came to the station we did not part company, and Gray seemed quite pleased when we all entered the same compartment.

On the journey I had no newspaper and decided to go over the case and suspects again in my own mind to see whether I could reach a new conclusion. Great murder cases of the past threw little light on this one for it was hard to see how it resembled any of them as yet. If Rudolf was guilty it might have something in common with the Thompson and Bywaters Case, for I was prepared to agree with Mrs. Gabriel that if Rudolf murdered Cosmo, Freda Ducrow had had her part in it. If Mills was the murderer—and I had an obstinate feeling that he might be—the whole thing most nearly followed the Rattenbury Case, including the wife's drinking and hysteria. If any of the women had killed Cosmo Ducrow it would mean something almost unprecedented for I could think of no murder by a woman in which there had been such horrible, such wanton violence.

I was turning all this over in my mind and had begun to grow drowsy as I went over the list of suspects, like a man counting sheep, when suddenly I heard Beef say something which made me sit bolt upright and become very wide awake.

"You know where we're going, don't you?" he asked Gray, and without giving him time to reply blundered on. "We're going to see the girl whom Major Gulley had with him that evening. You see, Mr. Gray, there's a great deal about Major Gulley's movements on the night of the twelfth which needs explaining."

"He has told you that he spent the night at the flat. The hall-porter saw him."

"The hall-porter saw him come in with the girl and saw him again next morning. He did not see the girl go. He cannot say that Major Gulley did not go out to take her home then drive straight down to Hawden."

"That sounds preposterous. What makes you suggest it?"

"Just that his car was in Hawden early that morning."

"You have evidence of that?"

"Moreover, it was at what has been called the scene of the crime."

"So that's what you have been referring to in all this talk about a car. But have you any reason to suppose that Major Gulley was driving it?"

"I've no proof that he was," said Beef. "Perhaps I shall know better when I have seen Miss Esmeralda Tobyn."

It was fortunate that we had the carriage to ourselves. Gray was flushed and angry.

"I employed you to find out who had killed Cosmo Ducrow," he said, "and so to clear his nephew of suspicion. All you have done so far is to give the police something which they take for further evidence of his guilt and stir up a lot of dirty water. What business have you to be seeing this... lady?"

"Dirty water," Beef retorted sadly, "is frequently all I find when I come to go into a case like this. Especially when in one household there are two people who have been in prison."

Gray suddenly ceased to be righteously indignant and gaped at Beef as though appalled.

"*Two?*" he gasped.

"That's what I said. If not more," he added.

Gray waited a long time before answering. At last he said in steady solemn tones: "Sergeant Beef, I believe you to be an honest and a well-intentioned man. I ask you, for everybody's sake, to clear up this terrible business as quickly as you can. None of our nerves are of iron, and I for one cannot stand much more."

"I have told you all along—I'll do my best, Mr. Gray."

Seeming quite satisfied with himself, Beef lit his pipe and picked up his newspaper.

15

As the reader may have guessed, the address 18 Peckham Avenue, Putney Common is an imaginary one. I have invented it to avoid revealing where Miss Esmeralda Tobyn was living at this time, for the owners of the house in which we found her may have been totally unaware of the somewhat disreputable character of the place. Suffice it to say that it was in one of the south-western postal areas, a large building which may once have been the home of a Victorian city man and was now a honeycomb of small flats and apartments.

On the second floor we found the name for which we were looking, written on a postcard which had been pinned to a door. Beef gave a peremptory knock.

I was expecting Miss Tobyn to be as raffish and slatternly as the house, but it was a neat well-dressed young woman of about twenty-eight who opened the door. I saw that she was rather attractive and she showed no signs of flurry or dismay on seeing two strangers.

"Good morning," said Beef. I thought at first that he would be content with this greeting and not add one of his tactless crudities, but I was mistaken. "I've come about the murder," he said.

Miss Tobyn remained motionless. She showed no disposition to bluster or panic. She did not cry "What murder?" or dramatically ask what any murder had to do with her. She simply waited.

"I understand you were with Major Gulley that evening."

"I've gone into all that with Chief Inspector Stute."

"I know you have. But I have been retained by the family to make some further enquiries, and there are a few questions I should like to ask you. My name is Beef. This is Mr. Townsend."

"Come in, then."

We entered a sitting-room from which another door led into a bedroom, I guessed. The room was quite nicely furnished, and I noticed some fresh chrysanthemums on a table.

"This is really rather a bore," said Miss Tobyn. "I scarcely knew the man."

"Who? Ducrow?"

"No. No. I never met any of them. I mean the man you call Gulley."

"What did you call him?"

"He told me his name was D'Agincourt and that he worked at the B.B.C. It seemed quite likely. If there was a man called D'Agincourt he almost certainly would work at the B.B.C., and the voice sounded familiar, somehow."

"I know what you mean," admitted Beef. "How long had you been acquainted with him?"

"About three months, I should think."

"Where did you meet him?"

"At a club called the Surly Tapster. I was told he positively haunted the place."

"Seemed to have plenty of money?"

"Bags of it. Needed it, too, with a moustache like that."

"You found him unattractive?"

"Actually, no. I found him rather a cup in a bizarre sort of way. And madly generous."

"You spent a number of evenings with him?"

"Yes. Perhaps a dozen in all."

"But he never mentioned that he lived in Kent or that he was employed as secretary and agent by Mr. Cosmo Ducrow?"

"Never."

Beef had been talking rather casually. Now he rounded on Miss Tobyn and snapped out his next question.

"When did you first hear the name Ducrow?"

"Er... I suppose when it appeared in the newspapers."

"Major Gulley never mentioned it?"

"No."

They stared at one another defiantly. At last the tension was broken by a suggestion from the young woman that we should have a drink.

"I don't mind," said Beef and watched her bring bottles from a cupboard.

"You'll excuse me asking," said Beef clumsily, "but have you got some job or profession, Miss Tobyn?"

She smiled.

"This house *does* give a bad impression," she said. "I have a small income of my own and I have a job."

"May I ask what?"

"Floristry."

"What, wreathes and that?"

She looked to me for sympathy, and I felt impelled to explain.

"Really, Beef, there are times when you show yourself lamentably ignorant. The art of flower arrangement has gone far beyond 'wreaths and that', as you put it, and has become a full-time occupation for many talented people. Miss Constance Spry has founded a school..."

"You mean, just how to arrange flowers in vases?"

Miss Tobyn smiled.

"If you like. Anyway that's my job. I live here because I can find nowhere else. It's not really quite so tartish as it looks."

Beef coughed and picked up his notebook.

"Now we come to the night of the twelfth," he said severely.

"Need we? Really? I have told the police all that."

"Not quite all, Miss Tobyn, surely? At what time did you meet Major Gulley?"

"He called for me here in that old chariot of his. About seven, I think. We had a drink here and left some time after eight."

"Where did you dine?"

"At the Cochon d'Or."

"Decent grub?"

"The Cochon d'Or has probably the best cuisine in London," I tried to explain to Beef.

"All right. All right. What then?"

"Then, Sergeant Beef," said Miss Tobyn with understandable defiance. "I accompanied Mr. D'Agincourt to his flat in Montrevor House."

"How long were you there?"

"I'm sorry. I'm *not* a time-table and I do not book down my movements."

Beef was unruffled.

"All right. Say three or four hours. What then?"

"Mr. D'Agincourt drove me home."

"Whose home?"

"I don't understand what you mean."

"I think you do, Miss Tobyn. What's more, for everyone's sake, I think it would be best if you told me the truth now." The girl was silent. The light from the window was full on her and I thought she looked rather beautiful as she stared at Beef with round troubled eyes. Her hair was of an unusual shade of chestnut, and she had very good teeth. I remember that during those few moments I was hoping that she was not going to become deeply involved in this case.

"As a matter of fact," she said slowly, "I wanted to do so a long time ago but Poppy d'Agincourt was against it. He said there was no need for anyone to know, ever, and he didn't want me dragged in. He's rather an old pet, really, though I wouldn't trust him far in money matters."

She then told us a surprising story. Gulley, or Poppy as she called him, had told her about the cottage he was going to move into and had suggested some time ago that she should come and live there. It had two acres which could be used for intensive flower-growing, and she had long had the idea of moving out of town and growing her own flowers then perhaps opening a tiny shop somewhere in the West End from which she could get orders for flower decorations. Gulley had promised her to build a glass-house.

At this point Beef interrupted to ask rudely which of them was married already, to which she replied that actually both were, but Gulley's wife was in South Africa and she had not seen her husband for years.

On the night of the 12th, as they were walking to the car from Montrevor House, Gulley suddenly had an inspiration and asked why she did not drive down with him now and stay in the cottage for a few days to see how she liked it. She had no engagements for the next two days and liked doing things on impulse. In a few minutes they were in the Lagonda on their way to Hokestones. They must have left London, she thought, at about three or half-past.

During the last twenty miles of their journey they had the road entirely to themselves until they were approaching the village of Hawden. Then they saw a young policeman in uniform pushing a bicycle. They entered the drive because, although there was another road to the cottage, Gulley had to get the keys from his room. They were going to stop some way from the house while he slipped in to get them. But when they came round a bend of the drive the headlights of the car showed them what looked like a man lying on the ground beside a seat and near a small pavilion.

Miss Tobyn faltered a little here, and I could see that she was greatly distressed by the recollection of what had taken place. It appeared that Gulley had no torch, but left the headlights of the car on while he went across to investigate. When he came back he was in what she now described as a "dreadful state". He told her it was Cosmo Ducrow, his employer, and that he had been murdered. The back of his skull had been smashed right in—a horrible sight.

She begged him to go straight to the police. She wished now that she had made him do so. But Gulley did not want her drawn into this. Besides, as he said, he was in some kind of trouble with Ducrow and might be suspected himself. When she pointed out that she could give evidence to confute any suggestion of that, he had grown all the more panicky and said they must drive straight back to London. He would take her to her flat first then get into Montrevor House without being seen and no one would know they had been anywhere near Hokestones.

They drove back very fast. She saw the policeman again but did not expect him to be able to identify the car. She supposed the police must have traced her by making enquiries at the Surly Tapster. That was really all. It was perfectly certain that Gulley could have had nothing to do with the murder for he had never been out of her sight that evening.

She took a long stiff drink of gin and tonic and sat back to wait for what Beef would say.

Beef, however, had become cagey, and after muttering "Very interesting," or something of the sort, seemed engrossed in his notes. He only asked Miss Tobyn one other question.

"Can you play croquet?"

"Used to, when I was a kid," she replied. "It must be years since I've had a mallet in my hands."

Just then the telephone rang and she picked up the receiver, which was in the room we occupied, close to me. I could catch some of the caller's words as well as her own and soon gathered that it was Gulley. He had discovered or guessed that we were coming to see her and had phoned to beg her to say nothing, but she admitted that she had already told us. "I'm sure it's best," she added. Gulley evidently did not think so and there was a long argument during which Beef helped himself to another drink.

When we had left the house Beef said gravely: "I think we had better get back to Hawden as soon as possible."

I pointed out that I must call at my flat and he remembered that he had intended to go home.

"But I don't want to be away longer than we can help," he said. "I wouldn't like to be responsible for what may happen if we're not on the spot."

This seemed to me to be rather self-important, and I suggested that we should go down the following morning.

"No, no," said Beef impatiently. "This evening at the latest. What time is there a train?"

I can never be quite sure with Beef. He was capable of dragging me back sooner than I wanted to go merely so that he could play in some wretched game of darts. On the other hand, there might be genuine urgency in the matter.

"There's a good train at ten-four," I said. "I'll meet you at Victoria."

That seemed only partially to satisfy him, but he made no further protest.

"How did you know she was with Gulley at Hokestones that night?"

"I didn't, for certain. But why else should he have driven back to London? That is, if there's any truth in the story at all."

16

It was nearly midnight when we came to Hokestones, but we found lights on and a great state of perturbation. Gabriel broke the news to us as soon as we came into the hall.

"She's gone," he said.

"What do you mean? Who has gone?" I asked him severely.

"Mrs. Ducrow. I'm not surprised myself. I thought she had more to do with it than what anyone seemed to believe. She drove down to Folkover today, saying she was going to see a lawyer. She was to have met Gulley at six o'clock but never turned up. Nothing heard of her since. Caught the eleven o'clock channel steamer and hopped it. That's my bet."

Beef clearly disapproved of this wild and speculative talk and pulled Gabriel up with a straight question.

"Where were you this afternoon?"

Gabriel seemed baulked for a minute, then, as though deciding to bluff it out, said loudly: "In Folkover, as a matter of fact. Often go down there on my day off."

"Where are Mr. Gray and Major Gulley?"

"Major Gulley's in the library. Mr. Gray's not back yet."

We found Gulley ostensibly in great distress.

"I can't understand it!" he said. "Mrs. Ducrow asked me to come down today and meet her after she had seen her solicitor. I was to wait for her at the Marina Palace. She expected to be there soon after six o'clock. I waited till nine and there was no sign of her."

"Have you been on to the solicitor?"

"Yes. At once. Mrs. Ducrow was with him for about an hour. He did his best to reassure her, and thinks he succeeded. She was calmer when she left him than when she arrived."

"What does Mr. Gray think about this?"

"He doesn't know yet. He phoned through this evening to say he is spending the night in the London flat and seeing Sir Mordaunt Tiptree in the morning."

"Haven't you phoned him?"

"Not yet. I've only been back about half an hour. I went to the police station in Folkover and asked them to do what they can."

"I think Mr. Gray ought to be told. What is the telephone number at the flat? You phone him, Townsend."

I was soon through and explaining the matter to Theo Gray. At first he did not quite see the seriousness of it. He suggested that Mrs. Ducrow might have decided that she did not want to meet Gulley and was making her own way home. She might have stopped on the way, he said, and reminded me of her "little weakness". I pointed out that Mrs. Ducrow was a very highly strung lady and in a state of great anxiety and distress. For anyone in her state of mind to be missing, even for a few hours, was cause for great alarm and I underlined my meaning by reminding Gray of her frequent threats "if anything happened to Rudy". Gray would not hear of it. Women talked like that, he said sweepingly, but Mrs. Ducrow was not the type to do anything silly. Finally I tried to suggest the possibility voiced by Gabriel of her having decided to cross the Channel. Gray was silent at that and said finally that nothing more could be done tonight and that he would cancel his appointment with Sir Mordaunt Tiptree and come down by an early train in the morning.

This did nothing to calm Gulley.

"It's all very well for him to say she's not the type," he said. "Freda might do anything. She's very much in love with Rudolf, and if she thinks they're going to arrest him she is capable of any lunacy."

Beef, as usual, damped this excitement by a question.

"What time did you get to Folkover? he asked.

"Earlier than I expected. The accountant left at about three and I went straight down. I did some shopping and had tea at the Taj Mahal."

"You saw no one you knew in the town?"

"No."

I thought I had never seen a man change so quickly as Gulley had in these few days. The boisterous individual with the bald head and monstrous moustache who had greeted us so heartily on our arrival had become a sagging and weary man. Even the moustache looked lifeless.

"What time did you leave Folkover?" went on Beef relentlessly.

"I don't know. About half-past ten, I think. I supposed I should find her back here."

"The police have a full description of her and the index number of her car?"

"Yes. I gave them everything. They promised to phone when they had news. Look here, Beef, this woman has been very good to me. Whatever may be said about her she was kind..."

"All right. All right. There's no need to think the worst yet."
Gulley poured three fingers of whisky into a glass and
drank it neat.

"No one's asked me to have a drink," said Beef reproach-
fully.

"Sorry. Help yourself. I hear you've been to see Esmé
today?"

"I've seen Miss Tobyn, yes."

Encouraged by the whisky he had drunk, Gulley now
became more confident and spoke loudly.

"Well? Do you blame me for what I did? There was no
reason to drag her in. Cosmo was... very dead."

"You examined the body."

"Examined?" shouted Gulley. "One look was enough.
You've never seen such a sight."

"Haven't I?" said Beef reflectively. "You might be surprised
at some of the things I've seen. However, you took one look
and then went back to the car? You didn't even notice the
croquet mallet lying there?"

"No. Nothing. I saw... what remained of Cosmo and it
was enough for me."

"Was Cosmo going to prosecute you?"

Gulley gave us a glassy look of embarrassment, but
answered quietly.

"No. I don't think so. I'd admitted the whole wretched
thing."

"In fact, until this happened today you were sitting pretty.
An alibi for the night of the twelfth..."

"What do you mean, 'until this happened today'? I simply
went to meet Mrs. Ducrow as she asked me and waited there
hours for her. The barman knows I was there."

"Thinking of another alibi, Major Gulley?"

"Good God! What for? You don't suppose Freda has been *murdered* do you?"

"It is one of a number of possibilities. But probably the most remote. Now I'm going to find out one or two things."

I followed him through the hall to the kitchen quarters. We found the Gabriels in their sitting-room but there was not quite the spontaneous welcome for Beef of the former occasion.

"Come in," said Gabriel wearily. "What is it this time?"

"Did Mrs. Ducrow take any luggage with her today?" he asked Mrs. Gabriel.

"No. Not that I saw. I could soon run upstairs and see if anything's gone, though."

"I wish you would."

"Why don't you leave it alone, Sarge?" asked Gabriel. "Look what a mess it's turning out. Now the poor woman's had to skip to the Continent."

"I've told you that's guesswork. And why has she *had* to skip?"

"Because she's scared."

"Oh, you think the police suspect her?"

"There's other things to be scared of besides the police. I'm scared myself."

"What of?"

"I don't know. I don't like this place. There's something very nasty about."

"You mean a murderer?"

"Not just a murderer. Crippen was a murderer and wouldn't have scared a child. I can't explain what I mean. It's in the air. You feel as though you're being watched."

"You are. Everyone concerned is."

"I don't mean that either. I've got the feeling that one wrong step and I've had it. Same as the old man had."

Just then Mrs. Gabriel returned to say that she was certain no baggage, or anything, had been taken by Mrs. Ducrow.

"Her toothbrush and her diamonds are there and she wouldn't have gone far without them."

"Well, thanks again, both of you," said Beef. "Now I'm just going to have a word with Mills. Good night."

The chauffeur was stretched on his divan bed, half-dressed, reading.

"Where've you been all day?" asked Beef.

"Nowhere much. Didn't go out till nine o'clock. Thought you would be down."

"Did you take Mrs. Ducrow's car round for her today?"

"Yes. After lunch."

"Any luggage with her?"

"No."

"Say what time she'd be back?"

"No. Told me not to wait."

"You been driving this evening?"

Mills looked up, then grinned.

"Took the old man's car when I went to the local. Testing the engine."

"I see. Good night, Bomb."

Before we returned to the house, however, Beef asked me whether my car was still at the front door. When I said it was, he told me he wanted to run down to the lodges. He explained that if Mrs. Ducrow had disappeared the first thing the police would want to know was where Rudolf had been at the time. This seemed reasonable, and although I was longing to get to bed I agreed to accompany him.

I did not, however, bargain for another of his pieces of mysteriousness and play-acting. It was too late at night and the day had been too exhausting for that, and when we reached the bend in the drive near the little pavilion and he asked me to stop I felt inclined to ignore the request. He said it was a matter of the greatest importance so, *faute de mieux*, I stopped. Beef produced a torch and invited me to accompany him. I switched off my engine and followed him across. From the doorway he threw the light of his powerful torch round the pavilion.

"They've gone," he said in an awed voice.

"Who have?"

"The coat and hat have gone."

I could almost have screamed with exasperation when I realized that he was being funny at my expense.

"Look here, Beef," I said, "this is a serious case. You heard what Gabriel said? There is something dangerous here which you cannot define. Don't please be a buffoon again. I'm willing to follow you and I believe you know what you're doing. It's when you're funny that I find it unendurable."

"Sorry," said Beef. "Let's get on then."

We drove down to the lodge gates in silence. It was a very dark night and when I had turned out the car-lights I was glad of Beef's torch to see our way across to Rudolf's front door. The house was in silence and darkness and there was no reply to our knocking. Supposing that Rudolf and his wife were in bed and asleep we knocked louder.

After some minutes an upper window was opened in the lodge opposite and Mrs. Dunton's head was thrust out.

"They're not back," she shouted. "They've been away all day and taken the dogs with them. The police have been here for them tonight but couldn't get any reply."

"Thank you."

"Must have gone on foot," went on Mrs. Dunton who once having started to give information knew no way of stopping, "him not having his car."

"Thank you. Thank you."

"Never been as late as this before. With the dogs, too."

"Good night."

"Long time since they've gone anywhere together ..."

We moved away in the darkness, but Mrs. Dunton's voice followed us to the car, saying that she had seen them go out in the morning and was sure she would have noticed if they had returned.

17

I passed a restless night. It seemed to me as I fretted through the small hours that everyone was taking the disappearance of Freda Ducrow very calmly. I admitted that there could be quite ordinary explanations for it; she might for instance have decided not to meet Gulley and started to drive home, then stopped at some pub for a drink and having had too much for safe driving, have stayed the night. But it did not seem likely. Why should she have decided suddenly not to keep an appointment she had made only a few hours earlier? And would not the publican, in such a case, have found out who she was and telephoned? If her car had been involved in an accident we should have heard already.

Far more likely, I thought, that she had done the very foolish thing which Gabriel suggested—escaped to the Continent. Only someone in her state of nerves and unhappiness could have done something so stupid, for whether or not she was involved in the murder of Cosmo Ducrow it would avail her nothing.

It was at times like this that I found Beef most lethargic and exasperating. Surely Freda Ducrow's absence should be of the deepest concern to him? Yet last night he had seemed to take it almost as a matter of course. I felt he should be *doing* something about it, not saying "Ah!" and "Well!" in his bumbling way.

At breakfast the silence became intolerable. Gulley ate nothing and I no more than a piece of toast, while Beef munched sausages and drank several cups of tea.

"No news?" he asked when he had finished.

Gulley looked at him with disgust, and I said nothing.

"Ah, well, I expect we shall hear something soon."

Gray walked into the room soon after nine, having come down on an early train. He seemed to take Beef's side and remarked cheerfully that he was sure Mrs. Ducrow would be home soon, or that we should hear from her.

"Old Wickham is a very sound chap and will have given her good advice. I'm sure she won't have done anything rash."

Gulley suggested that Gray should at least phone the solicitor to ask whether Freda had made any remark during their interview which might throw light on her subsequent actions, and Gray, rather as though he were humouring us, agreed to do so. When he came back from the phone, however, he had little to tell.

"She seemed quite calm when she left him. He got the impression that she was more upset about poor Cosmo's death than she had shown. She was really very fond of him. But of course her main anxiety was over Rudolf. He was able to reassure her on that score. She seemed almost cheerful when their interview ended, and asked old Wickham to come out here and see her soon."

"Yes," said Gulley. "But we all know how volatile she was. She might have changed her mood completely within an hour of leaving him. I think the best thing I can do is to go down to Folkover."

"I can't see what good that will do."

Just then the telephone rang and in a few minutes Gabriel came in. We all looked anxiously towards him, but it was Beef whom he summoned.

"Inspector Stute on the phone," he said.

Beef was out of the room for only a few moments but when he returned I could see that at last he was disturbed.

"Stute's on his way up," said Beef. "He says he has grave news for us."

"Does that mean she is dead?" shouted Gulley. It was not pleasant to hear the hysteria in that usually lush and confident voice.

"I don't know what it means," returned Beef. "Mr. Gray, I think it would be as well if Mr. Rudolf Ducrow were present."

"Of course. I'll phone him."

I was surprised when a few minutes later Gray returned to say that Rudolf was on his way up.

"He must have returned very late last night," I observed.

I could see that Beef would have preferred that I should have kept this observation to myself. Gray turned to ask me what I meant and I related the story of our late and fruitless call at the lodge. No one seemed much pleased by this.

When Rudolf came in I felt inclined to ask him a few tactful questions about yesterday, since no one else seemed to think this necessary, but as soon as I turned to him I heard Beef clearing his throat in a marked manner and gathered that he had some reason for wishing me to say no more.

Gray gave Rudolf what information we had about Freda and I was astonished to notice that he, too, seemed unperturbed at first.

"After all, it won't be the first time she has gone away unexpectedly," he said. "You remember that occasion on which she suddenly went up to London and stayed the night without telling Cosmo? He was frantic about it."

But when Gray came to the message from Stute, Rudolf also became serious.

"Sounds bad," was all he said, however.

Stute came in with Liphook and I could see from their faces that the news they brought was indeed grave. At least, I thought, it would be broken tactfully, for Stute is a man of breeding and would not blunder into an announcement of tragedy as Beef so often did.

"I'm afraid I have very bad news for you all," he said.

We waited in silence. I could see that even he, who had investigated so much crime and dealt with so many terrible situations, hesitated now.

"It's about Mrs. Ducrow," he went on quietly. "I am sorry to have to tell you that she is dead."

"Good God!" It was Gulley who exclaimed, and I saw that he was pale and trembling.

Gray spoke quietly.

"Will you please give us the details?"

"They are very tragic. This morning at seven o'clock a coastguard named Richard Pugh saw something which looked like wreckage on the beach near Greynose Head. He was on the cliff at the time and could only make out a dark shape beneath, but he decided at once to investigate. High tide last night was at seven forty-five and it would be high tide again at eight twenty-three. He hurried down to the gap and raced along the beach to get to the wreckage before the sea reached it and in time to return to the gap before he was himself cut off. He knew that he had only just time to do this, and did not wait to summon anyone.

"He found the wreckage to be that of a Hillman Minx car, Number GSG 117, which as you know was Mrs. Ducrow's. In the wreckage, badly mutilated by the fall and quite dead, were the remains of the unfortunate lady. It was evident that the car had been driven over the edge of the cliff.

"Pugh had only time for a brief examination of the wrecked car and the corpse, but he is certain that the sea had not come up to it. At this point and at this time of year the water reaches the foot of the cliff but does not rise high on its face. Since the car was only a few yards from the cliff it must have been driven over at some time after about nine o'clock on the previous evening."

I looked round the strained and serious faces about me, but learned nothing from them. There was a tense silence as Stute continued.

"Beside the lady was a broken bottle in the remains of which were still a few drops of whisky. Also her bag in which, since then, has been found a sum of money in Treasury notes.

"The coastguard did the best thing possible in the circumstances. The tide was approaching fast now and he had only time to extricate the body from the wreckage and by an effort, which must have been considerable and for which he merits praise, carry it to the gap. It is now being examined."

"What about the car?" asked Beef.

"Inspector Forster has gone down and will make an examination as soon as he can reach it. By then, of course, the sea will have been over it."

Gulley seemed bewildered.

"Do you mean that Mrs. Ducrow committed suicide?" he asked.

"I do not mean any more than I have said, Major Gulley. Her car was driven over the edge of the cliff with her at the wheel sometime after, say eight forty-five last night."

Gray spoke rather fiercely.

"I do not believe that Freda Ducrow would kill herself," he said.

"Why not, Mr. Gray?"

"She was not that kind of woman."

"But I understand that she has repeatedly threatened to do so?"

"She talked foolishly, but that's a very different thing."

"Then you think it was an accident or a murder?"

"I don't believe it was suicide. Have you any further information?"

"The tracks are quite clear where she left the road but they cannot be traced clearly across the springy grass of the downs. Nothing that she carried gives us much information. We have not yet been able to trace anyone who saw her car or her at any time yesterday evening." Stute turned to Rudolf. "Do you believe that Mrs. Ducrow may have committed suicide?" he asked.

"No. Frankly, I don't."

"You seem to be unanimous about that. It's strange that when a lady of her rather excitable nature, who is known to have drinking bouts and to be depressed and worried, is found in circumstances which point to suicide, you should be so sure that she did not kill herself. What do you think, Beef?"

Now was Beef's chance to show the keen intelligence and quick instincts with which I had always credited him. I wanted him to say something which would impress Stute and the others. But he shook his head.

"I don't know what to think," he moaned. "Upon my word I don't. Proper puzzler, isn't it?"

"By which I suppose he means that he is going to startle us presently," said Stute sarcastically. "Now, I should just like to know where you all were yesterday evening between, say, six and ten. Major Gulley?"

"You know. I've told you. At the Marina Palace till nine, waiting for Mrs. Ducrow. The barman will remember me. After that round at the police station."

"Mr. Ducrow?"

"I took a bus to Cinderhurst last night. Went to the pictures there."

"What time did you come out?"

"I don't know. After ten."

"How did you get home?"

"Walked."

"Arriving?"

"No idea. Past midnight."

"See anyone who would remember you?"

"Not that I remember. You wouldn't expect me to have an alibi though, would you, Inspector?"

"No," said Stute sharply. "Now, Mr. Gray?"

"I was in London yesterday."

"Oh, yes. I was forgetting. Where was Gabriel?"

"He was in Folkover. Came home on the last bus, the nine forty-five from there."

"Sergeant Beef?"

"At home. Having a row with the wife."

"Mr. Townsend?"

"What on earth have I got to do with it?"

"Nothing, I hope. But I'd just like to make the check complete."

"Oh, very well. I was in my flat in London."

"Alone?"

"Certainly."

"What about your wife, Mr. Ducrow?"

"I don't know. She left me yesterday. Took her dogs and went."

"Dear, dear," said Stute. "You none of you believe it's suicide yet none of you could have been anywhere near Mrs. Ducrow at the time. We shall have to see what the Coroner thinks."

18

B eef decided that we should go down to Folkover at once. "I could do with a sniff of sea air," he remarked. "And what about whelks, eh? Nothing better when they're fresh."

I reminded him that we were investigating two deaths, perhaps two murders, and suggested that his levity was ill-timed.

"No levity about it. You've got to eat, haven't you, murder or no murder."

To bring him back to the matter in hand I said it was a pity that the sea would have been over Freda's car before it could be examined, but he replied that he did not think it mattered. Even if anyone had been with her that evening he wouldn't have left any fingerprints or anything of the sort, and in any case the car would probably have most of the prints of the family and dependants on it. Mills admitted that it had not been cleaned for ten days. As for the body of Mrs. Ducrow—what could you learn from that? A body which had been in a small car falling several hundred feet on to the beach would in any case be battered almost beyond recognition.

"You mean, she may have been dead before the car went over?"

"I suppose she may. Shouldn't think she was, though."

"If you don't expect to learn anything from the car I don't quite see why we are going to Folkover."

"I told you. Sea air and whelks. Now let me think."

I drove on, with Beef remaining silent. I was painfully aware that the process which he called "thinking" was going on beside me; indeed I could almost hear the mechanism of his brain at work.

We had a good clear road and were making excellent time when I saw in the mirror that an unmistakable police car was following us. Instinctively I slowed down, though Beef pointed out that this was not a built-up area and I was well within my rights to be doing fifty miles an hour. The police car seemed to accelerate and passed us at a speed which gave me the sensation of going backward. Beef was chuckling inanely.

"Old Stute," he said. "Means to be the first one on the spot. Well, he's welcome to it."

We did not, in fact, see the Chief Inspector again that day for when we reached Folkover Beef asked to be taken not to the police station but to the office of Mr. Ernest Wickham.

"I don't know what you expect to learn from him," I said crossly, but stopped at a telephone booth to find out the address. "Shall I see if he'll give you an appointment?"

"No. We'll just turn up. He can't help seeing us then."

He was right, for after Beef had explained to a clerk that he was investigating the death of Mr. Cosmo Ducrow on behalf of the family, we were admitted to a large and airy office overlooking the sea—quite unlike the musty cubby-holes in which most solicitors spend their professional lives. Nor did Mr. Wickham look characteristic of his calling. He was a dressy little man in a well-cut grey suit with a button-hole and enviably well-laundered linen. I guessed him to be about sixty, quick of eye and movement, a lively and forceful type.

"I can give you twelve minutes," he said sharply.

"You've heard about Mrs. Ducrow of course?"

"I have. Tragic."

"Did you anticipate anything like that, Mr. Wickham?"

"Anything like what?"

"Well, suicide."

"Certainly not. Mrs. Ducrow was in a condition of nerves and distress, but nothing in her conversation led me to think that she contemplated taking her own life."

"Yet within a few hours she had apparently done so."

"Apparently," said Wickham, faintly stressing the word.

"What I would most like to know is whether you noticed any suggestion of fear in her."

Mr. Wickham hesitated.

"She was very much afraid for Rudolf Ducrow," he said at last.

"And for herself?"

"Not in the same way. She had nothing to hide so far as her husband's death was concerned. She was past caring about any unpleasant publicity over her relations with Rudolf. But fear of another kind—yes."

"She admitted that?"

"I can tell you almost word for word what she said, though these remarks were not made consecutively but at different times during our interview: 'I don't want to stay in that house. I am afraid. There is something I am afraid of all the time. No, I can't say exactly what it is. Cosmo was murdered by somebody who is still near me—I'm sure of that. If only I knew who it was. Perhaps I shall be the next.'"

"She said that?"

"She said just that. But she was a highly imaginative woman, of course."

"Do you think she was murdered, Mr. Wickham?"

"Surely that is more in your field than mine? I have told you that she said nothing to suggest that she was contemplating suicide, but with a woman of her character it can by no means be ruled out."

"Quite so. She left you at about six?"

"At ten minutes to."

"Did she say where she was going?"

"Yes. She was going to meet Major Gulley. Now is there anything else you wish to ask me?"

"Is there anything else you wish to tell me?" countered Beef.

"There is this. You were employed by Theo Gray to find out who murdered Cosmo Ducrow. You have not done so. If you had, Mrs. Ducrow would still be alive. I believe you have a reputation higher than your appearance warrants. It cannot be impossible to trace a killer. Why haven't you done it?"

"Oh, but I have, Mr. Wickham."

"You *know* who killed Cosmo?"

"Yes."

"Then why on earth don't you charge him or her?"

"I have my reasons."

"They cannot justify you in silence."

"I think when you know them you will agree that they do."

"I see. One more thing. If Mrs. Ducrow was murdered, was it by the person who killed Cosmo?"

Beef shook his head.

"No, Sir. If Mrs. Ducrow was murdered it was not by the person who killed her husband."

"All I can say is the quicker you get over this childish game of mystery and tell the police what you know the better."

"I've told the police everything I know. Good morning, Mr. Wickham."

I was not going to pander to what Wickham had so aptly called Beef's childish game of mystery, and walked in silence beside him to the car park. Here a most unprepossessing small boy with spindly legs, pimples, spectacles and a notebook announced to me that my car was issued in Birmingham in 1938.

"I am well aware of it, thank you," I said, irritated by the priggish little know-all.

"That one there came from Coventry last year."

"Please go away," I said, "and stop showing off the useless knowledge you get from number plates."

Beef, however, seeing my irritation, came up and gave the unpleasant youngster a grin.

"This your hobby?" he asked.

"Yes. See, I keep this notebook for all the cars that park here, then I know where they were issued."

"And what good does that do you?" I asked. "Even train-spotting is more intelligent than this."

"I like it," said the boy with a cocky look at me. "I can tell the other chaps."

"Doesn't that rather bore them?"

"The other chaps would like to do the same only their mums want them home. My mum's got a goitre. A wopper."

"I can perfectly understand your mum's not wanting you home."

"Were you here yesterday?" asked Beef.

"In the afternoon I was. Mum had a man coming to see her and told me to keep out."

"What time were you here?"

"All the afternoon after three. I saw a cyclist knocked off his cycle. He wasn't hurt though."

"Were you here at five?"

"Yes. I didn't go away till it was time to see the last programme at the Odeon at seven-fifteen."

"Did you write down the cars that were in this parking place yesterday afternoon?"

"Course I did. I've got them all here."

Beef almost snatched the notebook from the boy's grubby hand and examined the entries for the previous day.

"Yes, here it is," he said to me, pointing to the index number of Freda Ducrow's car. "What are these numbers here, 505 and 557?"

"Times it came and went. Then I know how long it's been here."

Beef pulled out a two-shilling piece.

"What's your name?" he asked.

"Mine? Leonard Parks."

"Well, Leonard, I think that's a very useful hobby of yours. You'd better buy yourself a new notebook and pencil with this."

"You might make it half-a-crack," said the odious boy. "Then I can get an indelible pencil."

Looking less amiable, Beef pulled out another sixpence.

"Don't forget your car came from Birmingham in 1938," shouted the boy as we drove away.

"Where now?" I asked.

I might have guessed the answer.

"They're open, aren't they?" said Beef as if aggrieved at my slowness of comprehension in failing to guess what he wanted. "Besides, we can combine business with pleasure. Drive to the Marina Palace."

The cocktail bar at the Marina Palace, the only bar entered from the hallway of the hotel, was called "The Smuggler's Den", but its decoration would have served equally well for the Buccaneer's Cave, Drake's Cabin, the Pirate's Saloon or the Armada Room, all of which I have discovered in various English hotels. I need scarcely describe the plaster carvings gilt and lacquered, the ship's models and the illuminated port-holes we found. Behind the bar, his head framed by a diploma for cocktail shaking, stood a most unpiratical barman who eyed Beef as though he was the man who had come to collect the garbage.

"Yes?" asked this pomaded youngster before we had finished balancing ourselves on two very high and uncomfortable stools.

"I'll have a pint of wallop..." said Beef.

"If you mean beer, Sir," the barman said, pronouncing the word as though it was burning acid on his lips, "I'm afraid we don't serve it here. You'll have to go out of the front door and round to the outside bar..."

"I shall have to do nothing of the sort, you cheeky young monkey," said Beef. "What's a bar for if there's no beer? This *is* a bar I suppose?"

"It's the Smuggler's Den," said the barman, and no name could have sounded more *outré* from his lips. "We have the bottled beer, of course, only you said 'wallop'. I understood that meant draught beer or something of the sort."

"I'll have a brown then," said Beef. "What's yours?" he asked me.

I had been studying the list of cocktails, and saw that the barman had won his award with one called The Kiss of Night.

I thought that since we wanted information from the barman it would be conciliatory to ask for this. Beef gave a low guffaw. "You'll get Kiss of Night!" he said. "Kiss my Aunt Fanny, I should call it."

The barman was huffed.

"It's very good," he said hotly. "A little gin, lemon juice, just a hint of Maraschino..."

"I'm sure it's excellent," I said. "Sergeant Beef does not appreciate anything but beer. Now, we wanted to ask you about last night. Did you have a man with a large moustache here?"

"Did I? I thought he'd *never* go. He came in just as I was opening up and stayed till after nine. He was the most *crashing* bore I've ever known. Kept talking about some lady he was expecting. Drank double gin and soda all the time—a most revolting drink. What did you want to know about him?"

"I think you've told us all we want to know. He stayed here all that time? Never went out?"

"Only to the Gents once or twice."

I suddenly noticed that Beef was making a violent show of impatience. "I've just thought of something," he whispered. "Finish your drink and come on. Quick! It's urgent."

19

"Whatever's the matter with you?" I asked Beef. "I was just getting details of Gulley's movements last night."

"Yes, but there's something urgent. Drive back to that car park as quick as you can. I can't think how I can have been so careless."

I obeyed, but when we approached the line of cars along the promenade Beef gave a grunt of disappointment for the small boy was no longer there. An ancient attendant with a bright and bulbous nose said that he had often seen the youngster but had no idea of his name or address. Sometimes, he added, the boy did not come for days on end, at other times you could not get rid of him.

"His name is Leonard Parks," said Beef hopefully, "and his mother's got a goitre."

"Got a goitre, has she?" said the car-park attendant, as though this might show him the light. "No. Can't say I know anyone with a goitre." An old man as crimson of face as he was now approached. "Know anyone with a goitre?" he asked.

"Can't say I do. Not with a goitre. There used to be a woman lived up Dell Hill way had a goitre but I haven't seen her lately."

"Name of Parks?" asked Beef eagerly.

"I couldn't say what her name was," said the old man severely, as though there was something improper in the suggestion that he might know her name. "But she had a goitre as big as an ostrich egg."

"Thanks," said Beef and gave him a coin. "I suppose we'd better try it," he added to me.

We found Dell Hill to be an area of rows of uniform houses, and stopped at a small general store in which we asked for news of Mrs. Parks. A number of women with shopping bags immediately went into conference, but it seemed in the end that none of them had heard the name.

"Got a goitre," put in Beef, but no light broke.

At last a woman who had remained silent said that there used to be a Mrs. Parks living in Lily Road at the other end of the town, but whether she had a goitre or not she wouldn't like to say.

In Lily Road everyone seemed just as anxious to help and just as unable to do so. No one knew anyone else with a goitre, and the name Parks meant nothing.

Beef tried mentioning the small boy with pimples and glasses who collected car numbers.

"There was a boy lived in Garden Avenue before I moved here used to do that," said an elderly lady, eager to help, "but I don't know if he wore glasses."

Garden Avenue turned out to be a short cul-de-sac not very far from the car park in which we had first seen the boy. There was no general shop here, but we were lucky, for a woman hurrying home with her basket knew Mrs. Parks and young Len and said they lived at number 17. When the door of this house was opened by a woman with a fierce and hostile stare and a magnificent goitre, we felt we were nearly home.

"Mrs. Parks?" asked Beef cheerfully.

"What is it?"

"It's about your little boy. I saw him this morning..."

"No you didn't because he's never been out of the house. Must of been some other little boy you saw, so it's no good your accusing my little boy because he's a good little boy and I haven't got the money to pay for any damage so you're only wasting your time and mine."

"He didn't do any damage," said Beef.

This piece of information seemed to flummox Mrs. Parks completely, and she stood gaping at Beef as though she couldn't believe her ears.

"What has he done, then?" she asked at last.

"Nothing wrong. It's some information we wanted. You see, he writes down all the numbers of cars in certain places..."

"I know he does. What do you want them for?"

Beef leaned forward and looked conspiratorial.

"I'm investigating a murder," he said in a hollow voice.

"And you mean to say something Len's written down will help you find out who's done it?"

"Very likely," said Beef.

"Then you don't get it not without he has his picture in the paper with his mother with him," said Mrs. Parks in a breath.

"I should have to see whether he's got the information I want first," said Beef.

Mrs. Parks raised her voice into a scream so sudden and shrill that it hurt my ear-drums.

"Len!" she called.

The boy came forward blinking.

"Is that the only car-park you do?" asked Beef.

"Course it's not. I do them all round there."

"Let's have a look at your notebook, then."

"No you don't. You're not to show it him, Len, till he puts your photo in the paper with your mother beside you. Now then."

The detestable little boy grinned at Beef.

"How much?" he asked.

"Ten bob," Beef told him.

"A quid," said the boy.

"You're not to do it, Len," said his mother.

"All right, a quid," said Beef. "Now come on!"

The notebook was produced and examined while Mrs. Parks raged unnoticed.

"Thank you," said Beef handing it back. "I've seen all I want."

"You little silly, you," said Mrs. Parks to her son. "You might have been on the television for all you know. Or in the newsreel, with your mum. Fancy showing it him like that. Now very likely someone'll be arrested."

We fled.

This time I was not to be taken in by any of Beef's mystification. I knew what he wanted to see and had seen.

"So Gulley's car was there?" I smiled.

Beef nodded.

"Until what time?"

"I don't know. The boy left for the cinema at seven. Now let's drive up to Greynose Point."

"Don't you want to go to the police station? They'll have reports about the body and the car by now."

"No. I can see those from Stute for what they're worth. I want to see where it happened."

It was a gusty but clear afternoon as we took the downland road from the town, winding our way upwards round sharp bends. After the last houses on the hillside there was nothing between us and Greynose Point except the Greynose hotel, a summer resort high on the headland. The whole distance from Folkover to the Point by road was about two and a half miles, but it was possible to cut across the downs, pass the hotel and reach the town on foot, and by this route the distance was under two miles.

The road, we found, did not go within five hundred yards of the Point, but we saw a policeman in uniform ahead of us, and on Beef's instructions I pulled up beside him.

"I'm a friend of Chief Inspector Stute," announced Beef. "I want to have a look round."

"The Chief Inspector will be up very soon," said the constable, "so you can ask him then."

It was clear that the policeman was on duty at the point where Freda's car had left the road, for there were tyre marks still visible in the soft earth by the roadside. We drove on a few yards and left my car while we went on foot across the short sweet downland grass towards the cliff. We soon saw a post recently stuck in the earth, and gathered that this marked the point at which the car had been driven into space.

"Mm," said Beef. "Not much to see, is there? If it did stop on the way you couldn't tell now. This grass is like rubber. Let's go over to the hotel."

Here we found everything closed and desolate, and had to ring the bell for a long time before anyone came. A seedy looking man who said he was the resident manager explained that during the winter only he and his wife and one barman remained in the building, and that the full staff would not return before Easter.

"Were you here yesterday evening?" Beef asked when he had explained the purpose of his enquiries.

"No. As a matter of fact the wife and I went to the pictures. Got back about ten o'clock. Later than we meant to. But George was here if you want to see him."

George was spruce and middle-aged and gave businesslike answers. No, he had noticed no traffic passing last night. He had gone to bed early because there was nothing else to do and the manager had his key. Time? Oh, about nine or soon after. He had put the outside light on, the one over the front door, so that the manager and his wife could see their way round from the garage.

After that? Nothing really. One man had passed the hotel—at about quarter past nine. That wasn't unusual. Even in winter people walked up here thinking one of the bars would be open. This man had come from the direction of the Point and had followed the track which led down to Folkover, passing right in front of the hotel. He had seen him from his bedroom window, which was in the front. He had just been opening his window before getting into bed when he had seen the man coming down towards the hotel.

What then, Beef asked, had made George notice the man?

"There was one rather funny thing about him," George said. "It was quite a fine night, not a drop of rain falling, but as the man came near the light of the hotel he stopped and put up his umbrella. Funny, wasn't it?"

"Very funny," said Beef gloomily.

"Then he walked past the windows of the hotel with it up. I couldn't see whether he put it down again."

"So you really did not see much of the man himself?"

"Nothing at all. Only his dark figure before he put his umbrella up."

"You don't think it could have been a woman?"

George considered this.

"Well, it had never occurred to me. I suppose it is possible if she was wearing trousers."

"Thank you very much," said Beef. "You've been most helpful."

That closed the interview.

I took a glance at Beef's face to see how he was taking this clear contradiction of his earlier pronouncement to Wickham.

"So Freda Ducrow was murdered," I said, "and by the same person as Cosmo."

"Think so?"

"It's becoming pretty obvious, isn't it? I know you don't want to think that this hiding under an umbrella is significant because it was I who first reported a case of it. But I don't see how you ignore it. On the night of Cosmo's murder Mills saw someone with an umbrella up trying to burn a croquet mallet. On the night when Rudolf's car was stolen I saw him or her again. And now a person with the same trick is seen coming away from the cliff over which Freda Ducrow's car has crashed."

"I still say that if Freda Ducrow was murdered it was not by Cosmo's killer. But there is one little piece of information I have kept back. I wasn't going to tell you because you thought you knew why I wanted to see that kid's list of cars. But fair's fair and you may as well have the same chance as I have of solving the case. Gulley's car was on his list—for the car park on the sea-front near the Marina Palace. But he covered another parking place, in a square near Wickham's office. And at four-twenty that afternoon Rudolf's car was parked there."

"*Rudolf's?*"

"You heard. Now you know as much as I do—though you may not have drawn the same conclusions from it. Let's get back to Hokestones."

20

I t occurs to me as I write this now that what Beef said was true—I *had* as much information as he had at that point, but I was completely bewildered, and all I could do was to make guesses at the identity of the murderer or murderers. What is more, I have scrupulously told the reader all Beef knew. As it afterwards transpired that Beef had now reached his solution, it seems to me that the reader may like to try his hand at finding the answers to the puzzle, and I am pretty confident that without cheating, without reading or looking into the remaining chapters, he will be no more successful than I was. I should therefore like to wager any reader a cigar that he cannot correctly fill in the spaces below:

Who killed Cosmo Ducrow?	
Was Freda Ducrow murdered, or did she commit suicide?	
If she was murdered, by whom?	
Who was the "person under the umbrella" when seen (*a*) by Mills, (*b*) by Townsend, (*c*) by George?	(*a*) (*b*) (*c*)

I own that I was baffled, but as we drove back I did not mean to give Beef the satisfaction of knowing this, and silently watched the road ahead.

It depressed me to be returning to that grey house and to the atmosphere of menace which I had sensed in it. Now, I thought, the murderer, whoever he or she may be, must be growing desperate, and desperate people are dangerous. Even Beef seemed to take this seriously, and warned me to keep my eyes open and look after myself for the next day or two. I asked him rather bitterly how I could do that when he did not even tell me from which quarter danger might come, but all he would say was, "From where you least expect it."

There was no sign of life in either of the lodges as we passed through the gates, and in the last light of evening the little croquet pavilion was no more than a black outline by the drive. Gabriel, opening the front door, looked surly and scarcely greeted us.

"Mr. Gray wants you in the library. He said, as soon as you come in."

As I anticipated, this meant an unpleasant interview with Theo Gray.

"Sit down," he said when we entered the library. "I think it is time we had a little talk. It seems to me, Sergeant Beef, that you should be feeling deeply concerned about the death of Mrs. Ducrow. Whatever its immediate cause, it would not have happened if you had done what you were employed to do and discovered Cosmo Ducrow's murderer."

"I'm sorry, Mr. Gray, but my methods can't be hurried."

"Your methods! I begin to doubt whether you have any. You surely must have known enough to see that the lady needed protection, either from herself or someone else? Yet on the day on which she met her death you had gone to

London on some wild-goose chase to interview a girl friend of Gulley's."

"I wouldn't call it a wild-goose chase, Mr. Gray. And after all, you went to London, too."

"I went because your dilly-dallying had made Rudolf's arrest seem imminent. I had to get him the best Counsel."

"I know. But I don't think you should blame me for not watching over the lady when you didn't think it necessary."

"The fact remains that the case is unsolved. Or do you yet know who killed Cosmo Ducrow?"

"I think I do."

"And Mrs. Ducrow?"

"Ah, that's another matter. But you wanted me to find out who killed her husband. Barring a few loose ends to be tied up, I think I have done so."

"Then why not charge him or her?"

"I've told you I can't be rushed. Now I want you to do something to help me get this over. Could you ask everyone concerned to be here tomorrow night?"

"What do you mean by everyone concerned?"

"Well, everyone who has any connection with this house or this case. Yourself and Gulley. Miss Esmeralda Tobyn."

"Really!"

"Well, she was in the grounds that night. Then Mr. Rudolf Ducrow and his wife…"

"His wife, I understand, is no longer at the lodge."

"Still, she could be sent for, surely. Then Mr. Ernest Wickham—that would complete the party above stairs."

"I suppose it could be arranged. What is the idea?"

"There are a few little questions I would like to ask them. Then outside, there's Mills and the Duntons as well as the Gabriels."

"You know, of course, that there has been a good deal of trouble between Mrs. Dunton and the Gabriels?"

"Yes. But I think it might be patched up for the occasion. I'll see to that if I have your permission."

"Very well. It all sounds rather as though you were making a play of it, I fear."

"Not really. I just need a little more information."

"I'll telephone Rudolf now," said Gray and left us.

Beef sat for a while in an armchair looking fixedly into the fire. When I tried to speak to him he made a shshsh-ing noise and said he was thinking. Then suddenly he jumped to his feet. His eyes were shining and he looked eager and boyish.

"Come on, T!" he almost shouted. Whenever he uses that abbreviated form of my surname I know that he is in one of his more mischievous moods, but I was glad to see that at last he intended some activity. "Come on! We must get to work!"

Infected by his wave of enthusiasm, I jumped up too.

"Right!" I said. "What do we do now?"

But I might have known.

"Run down to the local for a pint," he grinned.

I was furious at having been caught.

"You can go on foot," I said. "I'm not going to hang round a public house again while you guzzle beer."

"No one's asking you to. I want you to come in. No, straight up, T. We've got to see Bomb Mills. He'll be down there now. I need his help."

"The local" was not the country hotel at which Stute was staying, but a beerhouse on the edge of the village. Unwillingly I followed Beef into the public bar, reflecting that at least in this case I had not been dragged into one of these places as often as in Beef's previous investigations.

As usual, I found he had made himself known to landlord and customers alike and there were shouts of greeting as he entered. He acknowledged these with a wave of his hand, but when he had bought his pint and a glass of milk stout for me he made his way to the corner in which Mills was sitting alone, reading an evening paper.

"Hullo, Bomb."

"Hullo, Sarge. Got your man yet?"

"Not yet. I have hopes though. Couple of things I want you to do for me tomorrow."

"Well?"

"First of all, do you think you could get the Duntons up to the house in the evening? Drinks on me if it'll help."

"That won't be easy. You know what the two women are like."

"Still, you could work it. Bit of a reconciliation, perhaps? Say I need it for my investigations."

"I'll try. What's the other thing?"

"Have you got a steel cable for towing?"

"Yes."

"How long is it?"

"Fourteen or fifteen feet."

"Good enough. I'll tell you what I want it for tomorrow. I should like you to give me a hand then if we get the place to ourselves for a bit."

"Right you are."

"Now if you like to take the chalks while I get us another drink, we'll see the winners."

I knew that this offer presaged a long and dreary evening for me, spent in the smoky atmosphere of the bar, while Beef enjoyed himself playing darts. I was about to protest when I saw Rudolf Ducrow come in. He looked rather pale and tense, I thought, but this was not to be wondered at. There was no reason to doubt that he had been very fond of Freda Ducrow. He walked straight up to Beef.

"I was looking for you," he said. "I was told you were here. I scarcely expected it, though, within twenty-four hours' of Freda's murder."

"So you're another one who thinks she was murdered. Have you come to tell me that?"

"No. I came to tell you that I've got my car back. It was found outside Cinderhurst Station."

"When?"

"Apparently it was noticed at about midday today. The local police had been told to watch out for a car with that number, and one of them spotted it among the cars in the station yard which are left there every day."

"What was its condition?"

"Perfectly all right, as far as I could see."

"You don't know how many miles it has done since you drove it last?"

"I'm afraid not."

"All right, Mr. Ducrow. Thanks for telling me. Now, I'm on, I think."

"You mean you're on to the murderer?"

"No. No. On, I said. On the board. Waiting to play darts. Seeing the winners."

With a grunt of justifiable disgust, Rudolf flung out of the pub.

Not until closing time would Beef leave his favourite pastime. It appeared that he and Mills in partnership were able to defeat all challengers and so, as he put it, "stay on the board". He drank a great quantity of beer and grew noisy and pleased with himself. Then as closing time approached he became indiscreet enough to talk about the Ducrow case and boast that he had been too much for the murderer, as they would see in due course. I thought Mills looked rather uncomfortable then.

Nor would he go straight home, but insisted on calling at the Buck and Arrow to see Chief Inspector Stute. I tried to dissuade him because I thought it better that the Special Branch man should not see him in his present ebullient condition, but he maintained that the interview was essential.

Fortunately Stute had not gone to bed, and received Beef amicably. The two exchanged a certain amount of information, as usual making no comment on what each heard or said. Beef described his discovery of the young carspotter and its results and also, rather generously I thought, told the story he had heard from George. Stute, it appeared, had not neglected the Greynose Point Hotel and had already been given the same information by the barman. However, he showed Beef reports on the examination of Mrs. Ducrow's body and car. Beef's comment was that there was nothing new in these.

"I wanted to ask you," Beef said, "whether Inspector Liphook could come up to Hokestones tomorrow evening."

"What for?"

"I've arranged for everyone to be there. I should like him to witness something."

"Officially no, of course. I can't have the Special Branch dragged into your histrionics. But unofficially, if he would like to do so, I see no reason why he should not happen to be up there for some enquiries tomorrow evening. What time?"

"After they have their grub. Round about nine. He'll be with Townsend when the time comes."

"The time for what?"

"The time for him to witness what I want him to witness."

"Will there be any danger?"

"Not to him, there won't."

"Very well. I'll ask Liphook. It will be up to him of course. What exactly do you want him to witness?"

"Another murder."

"Indeed?" said Stute, evidently not taking this too seriously. "Who is going to be murdered this time?"

"I am," said Beef. "Only I'm not, if you see what I mean."

Stute smiled.

"I see what you mean," he said.

21

One might have thought, next day, that Beef was a General organizing a major offensive. He walked about with such an air of his own importance that I found him unendurable and left him as much as possible to himself. I noticed, however, that when Gulley and Gray left the house together, as they did during the morning apparently for a stroll, he hurried out to see young Mills. I did not think I should miss their interview, and followed him. To my surprise he did not seem pleased by this and turned on me rather tactlessly to explain that he had finished his investigations and that his plan of action was no concern of mine. He added ungraciously that if I wanted to know, he was going to get a length of steel cable, used for towing cars.

At lunch Gray informed us that he had been able to arrange for the presence this evening of all the persons mentioned by Beef, though Rudolf's wife, who was staying with her father, found it most inconvenient to come over. Gray hoped that these elaborate arrangements would be justified.

"I hope so, too," put in Gulley savagely. "I think it's disgraceful that Esmé should be dragged here. You know perfectly well that she had nothing to do with this affair."

Beef looked important and said that he could make no exceptions, and the subject was dropped.

After lunch he dragged me again to the kitchen, where the Gabriels were sitting over the remains of their lunch. There were no cheery greetings to Beef this time, however, and it was with resentful stares that they watched us enter.

"What have I done wrong?" asked Beef.

"There was no need to let them kill her like that," said Mrs. Gabriel, while her husband sat picking his teeth. "Either you didn't know better or else you could have stopped it and didn't. Whichever way it was, you don't know your job."

Uninvited Beef sat down.

"It wasn't my fault as you'll see when you know everything."

"When will that be? When the cows come home?"

"No. Tonight, if you'll help me."

"Help you? And you asking Gabriel where he was that afternoon as though he might have had something to do with it!"

"Come now," said Beef. "I've done nothing to hurt either of you. And you do want to find out the truth about all this, don't you?"

"Well, what is it you want?"

"I want you to have the Duntons up here this evening."

"What, '*er*?" shouted Mrs. Gabriel as though she were speaking of the Chaldean city. "You must be off your rocker. I wouldn't have her in this kitchen not if you was to offer me a thousand pounds."

"I'm offering you rather more than that," said Beef. "You want your share of what's left, don't you? Well, they can't do anything about the will till all this is cleared up."

"I'm not going to have her in my kitchen," said Mrs. Gabriel obstinately. "Besides, what do you want her here for?"

"I want all the suspects up here tonight."

"You mean to say she's a suspect?"

Mrs. Gabriel was evidently delighted.

"Yes; so is Dunton."

"Well, if you want them here because you suspect them, that's different."

"Only no trouble, mind," said Beef, following up his advantage. "I don't want them to think there is any unfriendliness between you."

"I'll see what I can do."

Beef sighed with relief, and soon we were on our way to see the Duntons. Here we were met at first with much the same decision. Wild horses, Mrs. Dunton said, would not drag her into the house again while "certain people" were still in the kitchen, still less persuade her to visit them. After all the mischief that "some" had made and the tales they had borne and the lies they had told she was surprised that Beef should even suggest such a thing.

Beef, undaunted, used tactics rather like those he had employed with the Gabriels. Things were coming to a head tonight, he said, and he wanted all suspects to be under observation. He could not, he pointed out, be in two places at once and while he was upstairs with the family he wanted someone to be with the Gabriels. Wouldn't Mr. and Mrs. Dunton undertake it for him?

Mrs. Dunton was persuaded. She would bring Dunton up at about eight o'clock.

"Though mind you," she added wistfully, "I wouldn't have my old job back not whatever they was to pay me."

From the lodge we went to look for Inspector Liphook as Beef said pompously that he wanted to "brief" him. We found him at the police station with Sergeant Eels and Constable Spender-Hennessy.

"Yes," said Liphook indifferently. "I'll come if there is going to be anything worth seeing."

Beef chuckled.

"You'll see all you want and a bit more," he promised.

Constable Spender-Hennessy lit a cigarette.

"Are you really going to stage one of these old-fashioned melodramas in which the detective demonstrates the guilty man before everyone else? It sounds about the last word in corn, but I should rather like to be there."

"Never mind what I'm going to do. Haven't you got your duties to attend to? What about turning-out time?"

"I can look after that if you want him," said Sergeant Eels.

"I don't want him!" shouted Beef angrily.

"Temper! Temper!" grinned Constable Spender-Hennessy. "What about when the guilty man pulls out a pistol and makes a last bold bid for freedom? That always happens, you know. 'Stay where you are, all of you!' he cries, edging towards the door. Wouldn't I be useful then?"

"I shouldn't think so," said Beef. "But if Inspector Liphook wants you with him I've no objection. Now Inspector, may I explain the layout? Where I want you and Mr. Townsend and this young man, if you bring him, is on the roof."

"Good gracious me," said Liphook. "Whatever for?"

"It's going to be a clear moonlit night. You'll be able to see everything from there. Now if you'll just look at this plan you'll see that the house has two sides to it, as it were, two wings, you might say, which are uniform in every respect. I've been up there this morning. I know.

"Each of these wings comes out a bit in front of the flat front of the house, and from each of them there is a way down into the house. So if you want to get out on to the roof of that wing you would go to the landing outside the Gabriels' room and go up by the little staircase there which leads to the attic floor. There you would find a set of wooden steps fixed permanently for anyone wanting to get out on the roof. Townsend knows where the Gabriels' room is and must have seen the staircase."

"Yes, I've noticed it."

"If you wanted to get to the roof of the other wing you would go along to Cosmo's old room at the other end of the passage and find an exactly similar staircase leading to the attic floor again where there is another set of steps leading to another door out on to the roof. I want you to go with Mr. Townsend to the Gabriels' end and get out on to the roof of that wing. You ought to be out there at 20.50 hours precisely."

"You're *not* going to say 'synchronize watches', are you? That would be too much." This was from Constable Spender-Hennessy, of course.

"Not a bad idea," said Liphook tactfully, and we all did as suggested.

"Any questions?" asked Beef.

"Yes. Is it possible to get from one wing to the other when you're out on the roof?"

"I was coming to that. Yes, it is possible. Round those chimney stacks. But I don't want you to do so until it's necessary."

"How shall we know that?" I asked.

"Put it this way. I only want you to cross from one wing to the other *in order to arrest a murderer.*"

"Oo-er!" said Constable Spender-Hennessy.

Beef ignored this.

"You'll know the moment for yourselves, if it comes. Any more questions?"

"Yes. What are we supposed to be watching for?"

"Developments," said Beef quickly. "Particularly on the other wing."

"I feel rather like a footballer," said Constable Spender-Hennessy.

"It's a pity you aren't one," said Beef. "Now…"

"Where do you want me and the Constable to be until we go out on the roof?"

"I'll leave that to Townsend. He will let you in at the best time and get you unseen into his bedroom. You can stay there till zero hour. I'll see if we can't get you a drink in there, but don't let anyone, staff or family, see you get in. And, Townsend, one point for you. Nothing cancels these arrangements. You understand? Nothing at all. Never mind what happens downstairs, unless I actually tell you, this arrangement stands. And for God's sake don't start using your own initiative or something. You get the Inspector and Constable into your room and then out on the roof at the right time and without being seen and you'll have done your part. Oh, and when you're up there don't let yourselves be seen. Get so that you can see across to the other wing without anyone seeing you. That's all."

With an unnecessarily loud snap of his notebook, Beef closed the conference and, clumsily playing for effect, made his exit.

I turned to the policemen.

"The best way for you to enter would be during dinner, I think. I could leave the french windows in the library open."

I then went into a detailed explanation of the geography of the house so that they could not make a mistake in finding my room.

"Your only danger during dinner is from Gabriel. There is a serving hatch from the kitchen to the dining-room so he is at that most of the while. But just be cautious as you cross the hall."

"Really," said Constable Spender-Hennessy, "this might be a detective novel."

I left them at that and hurried after Beef, catching him up as he walked slowly across the park. We decided to go in by the back way in order to tell the Gabriels the news about Duntons. As we crossed the yard we met Mills, dressed in a rather showy grey suit.

"Hullo, where are you off to, Bomb?" asked Beef.

"Cinderhurst. To meet my girl. It's my evening off."

"But you can't go today. I need you here."

"Sorry, Sarge. All fixed to take my girl to a dance. You seen her photo, haven't you? Well then..."

"Now listen, Bomb. You'll have to let her know you can't come tonight. You've got to be here. Everyone else is."

"I know, but you said it was for suspects. There's no reason why I should stay."

"I'm asking you as a favour. Besides, it would look very bad, wouldn't it? As though you had something to hide. You don't want to be involved in a lot more enquiries, do you?"

Mills hesitated.

"All right. I'll stay," he said at last. "It's a bind though. I'd been looking forward to tonight."

"There'll be plenty more nights for you, I expect," said Beef. As we walked away he said to me: "That's everything, I think. I hope there's no hitch. For your sake, and mine."

22

I would not willingly live through that afternoon again. Beef's ostentatious making of arrangements in preparation for what everyone supposed would be some sort of showdown had set us all on edge. Even Theo Gray, who had shown himself remarkably cool throughout the proceedings so far, seemed jumpy and bad-tempered, and Gulley looked as though he were seeing ghosts.

I realized that my own position was a difficult one. Whatever Beef's scheme might be, its success depended on my securing the co-operation of the two police officers, who were both rather sceptical about it. Nor could I rid myself of the notion that Beef might be playing to the gallery, and under some mistaken impression that he was providing me with a better story, be risking a fearful anti-climax. He seemed to be counting on the murderer behaving in a certain way, and that was surely a foolish thing to do. The man or woman who had been clever enough to kill one, and perhaps two, people under the very noses of a number of others would not walk into any trap clumsily set by Beef.

If he intended to expose the guilty person downstairs then expect him to make a dash for the roof, how could Beef know that the murderer would do anything of the sort? There were plenty of means of escape from the house; why should anyone be foolish enough to make for the roof?

Then the tow-rope. I imagined that to mean that Beef had some clumsy scheme connected with cars, if the murderer made a dash for it that way. Perhaps he and Mills had prepared something on the drive which would cause a car to be ditched. Beef's ideas were apt to be naïve, and I was prepared to find that he had worked out some elaborate nonsense which might fail to produce the effect he wanted. I only wished he would discuss these things with me, for my caution in them was an asset he lacked.

Then, at about a quarter to six and just as I was finding the strain unsupportable, Beef disappeared. I could scarcely believe that even he would go out to drink at such a time, but when I asked Gabriel where he was the answer left little doubt of it. Gabriel spoke with undisguised and understandable disgust.

"Where do you think? Young Mills has driven him off in the guv'nor's car. I heard him say he needed a livener."

This was too much for me, and I resolved to go and bring him back at once. I saw Cosmo Ducrow's Daimler outside the beerhouse in which we had spent yesterday evening and hurried in. I found him with a pint glass in his hand.

"Beef!" I whispered fiercely, "I'm not going to stand for this! With everything we have on our hands you can't come here and waste time. It's madness to drink when you need a cool head for tonight."

"Oh go away, for God's sake," said Beef rudely. "You're worse than an old woman. There's plenty of time before I have to show up, and I need a drink to steady me."

"There is not plenty of time. The guests are expected at any moment. You've arranged this party—you've got to be there."

"I'll be there all right, when the time comes. You look after your part of it and I'll look after mine."

"Don't you realize, you stupid fool," I hissed, "that your whole reputation depends on your handling of this?"

He suddenly looked quite serious.

"More than my reputation," he said. "My life, very likely. And perhaps yours. And others."

"Then come back at once!"

"I'll come back when I'm ready." He turned to Mills. "Nearest the middle for a start," he said and I could do nothing but show my disapproval by stamping out.

Yet, I thought as I drove back to Hokestones, yet there had been something in the way in which he said that his life and perhaps mine depended on his handling of this, something which was not buffoonery. Perhaps he really did need a drink to steady him, and his game of darts might be like Drake's bowls.

I remembered that Beef had promised the two policemen that there would be a drink in my room, and went to the library to see whether I could arrange anything. Among the bottles in a side cupboard I found a half-empty bottle of gin and was just holding it under my coat to see whether I could carry it through the hall without being seen when, most unfortunately, Zene Ducrow walked in. I was so embarrassed that I scarcely noticed that she was wearing slacks, and it was not until afterwards that I remembered George's remark about the person under the umbrella: "Well, it had never occurred to me. I suppose it is possible if she was wearing trousers." I tried to replace the bottle.

"Well, *well!*" she exclaimed in that unpleasantly loud and manly voice of hers. "A spot of secret drinking, what?"

I felt myself blushing.

"I scarcely drink at all," I said with what dignity I could. "I was just... I wanted to see..."

"Quite. Suppose you pour us out one each instead of sneaking away with it somewhere. What does your old Sergeant want us for this evening? A showdown, I suppose?"

"I really don't know. Sergeant Beef does not confide in me in these matters."

"It's a frantic bore. I've only come because I expect to see the murderer unmasked."

"Beef has made no promises," I warned. "He only says that he wants to ask a few questions."

"Who do you think murdered Cosmo?"

I was saved from the difficulty of answering by the entrance of Gulley with Esmeralda Tobyn. He quickly introduced the two women and hurried over to the drinks. I noticed that he poured out liberally for both himself and Esmeralda.

"This *is* going to be a cheery party!" said Zena.

"I only hope that at least it clears this horrible suspense," Gulley answered. "We can't go on much longer like this. If Beef knows who is guilty why can't he tell the police, instead of staging an elaborate *mise en scène?*"

"Perhaps the police know as much as he does," I conjectured, "but they cannot use his unconventional methods."

Gray came in with Rudolf—the latter looking remarkably steady and at ease considering the circumstances. When at last Ernest Wickham arrived our party was complete, with the exception of Beef.

"Where is the man?" asked Gulley.

"He's engaged at the moment. Something unexpected has turned up," I haltingly explained.

More drinks were poured and there were attempts at general conversation, but they were not very successful. I related a little anecdote about an uncle of mine whose raspberries were always disappearing until he discovered that they were being eaten by a retriever dog he owned. On previous occasions this story had held the interest of my audiences but tonight it had not its usual success. We all kept watching the door, expecting Beef to put in an appearance.

At seven o'clock there was still no sign of him and Gabriel, questioned, said that neither he nor Mills was back.

"I cannot think what is delaying him," I protested though unfortunately I knew too well. "I'm sure he will be here in a few minutes."

"I hope you're right," said Gray. "We have all taken great trouble to be here at his request, and unless it's a matter of life and death there is no excuse for his failure to arrive."

I saw an opportunity of defending Beef and looking as grave and mysterious as I could, I said: "I rather think it is—a matter of life and death."

This produced the silence I had anticipated. But I knew that I could not keep up this bluff for long, and when at half-past seven dinner was announced and still there was no word from Beef I made no further excuses but followed the party into the dining-room.

It was a strange meal. We sat and conversed and ate as other people were doing at such a small gathering as this, but with the sinister difference that one or more of those present, I reflected, might soon be facing retribution for a cruel, cold-blooded crime. One or more of those who ate the excellent roast pheasant which Mrs. Gabriel had provided, who tried to converse with his neighbour, must see in his mind's eye the frail figure of Cosmo Ducrow before the weapon had crashed down on the skull, must hear perhaps the last incoherent pleading of Freda Ducrow before she had been sent to her terrible death.

Perhaps if the guilty person was present he was trying to take some comfort from Beef's absence, as though this could save him.

"You find yours interesting work, Mr. Townsend?"

This was Esmeralda Tobyn who was on my right. I tried to make some sort of reply.

"Oh yes, indeed. It is not usually as nerve-racking as this. Beef's previous investigations have been just as... puzzling, but there has never been quite this anxiety before."

She looked at me for a moment and I thought there was something like sympathy in her attractive face.

"I suppose nothing could have happened to him, could it?" she asked.

This had never occurred to me. I have come to depend so much on Beef's burly confidence, his faculty for extricating himself from difficult situations created by his own impulsiveness, his undeniable strength both of muscle and character, that I had never thought of danger to him. Yet now I remembered his words about his life depending on his handling of the case and I felt a new fear.

"Oh no," I said as confidently as possible. "Old Beef can take care of himself."

But I had lost my assurance of this. I had left him with Mills, and both were drinking. I had never liked Mills or approved of Beef's friendly attitude towards the young man. At sixteen Mills had been convicted of burglary. Suppose that his story of the man with the umbrella was a lie, and he himself had murdered Cosmo. He had no alibi for that night, nor, so far as I knew, for the time of Freda Ducrow's death. In fact, as I remembered now, he had admitted taking the car out that evening. Had he realized that Beef knew too much? Was he, even now, guilty of a third murder?

Perhaps I ought to go and investigate? I could pick up Stute and we could perhaps trace them from the time they left the pub. Yet again I remembered Beef's emphatic instructions to me. "Never mind what happens downstairs unless I actually tell you, this arrangement stands." With such words there was no argument. I could only sit and pretend to eat and wait to see what might transpire.

The agonizing meal went on. Eight o'clock passed and at a quarter past there was still no relief. I had an additional anxiety over Liphook and Constable Spender-Hennessy, but since Gabriel had scarcely left the room I was fairly confident that they would have made their way safely to my room. I tried to listen to Esmeralda Tobyn talking about the arrangement of winter flowers on which she seemed to have the most revolutionary ideas, but could not concentrate.

Coffee was served at the table and Gabriel started to leave the room. Just as he was opening the door to go out I called him back, thinking that if by chance Liphook was crossing the hall just then this would warn him. For want of any better reason for having recalled Gabriel I asked him in a whisper to let me know as soon as Beef came in.

A few moments later he returned and told me, to my enormous relief, that the car with Beef and Mills in it had just come into the yard.

"He's having a wash at the kitchen sink."

I thanked him then announced triumphantly to Gray: "Sergeant Beef has come back. He will be here in a moment."

When the door opened we all looked across anxiously. With a sensation of sick horror I watched as Beef lurched stumbling into the room. His eyes looked glassy and his ruddy cheeks positively bloated. I saw at once that he was blind drunk.

23

The scene that followed was of course a painful one. The men and women gathered were, as I reflected, gentlefolk. Even if a murderer was among them they were people of breeding, and although they might have become accustomed to seeing a certain excess when Mrs. Ducrow was alive, yet the sight of Beef, stupefied with beer and stumbling towards a seat, to them could be nothing less than shocking. His voice was thick and he laughed too much.

"Sorry if I'm late for dinner," he said. "I've had my bit of bread and cheese already. The truth of it is this case has been a bit too much for me. Well, it is too much, isn't it?

"I was going to ask you all a lot of questions, but I don't think I will now. You'll only say it couldn't be any of you. Yet I know and you know and the police know that there's a murderer in this house."

"You're drunk," said Ernest Wickham.

"Little bit," admitted Beef with horrible coyness. "Just a little bit. Not drunk, exactly. Cheerful. I don't want to do any more work tonight though. I've worked hard enough on this case. And I've come to the conclusion that this murderer's going to be a bit too much for us. I don't see how we're ever going to get a conviction. I know who it is and tomorrow I'm going to make my report to the police. I hoped to substantiate it with a few things some of you could tell me tonight, but what's the good? You're all such nice people that you can't believe it of anyone you know. So I'm not going to ask you any questions at all. I'm going to bed."

His head seemed to droop forward and his eyes were half closed.

"This is a most disgraceful exhibition," said Wickham.

"Not really," went on Beef. "If you know as much about this case as I do you'd want to get drunk. Get drunk and forget about human nature for a bit. Mean, cunning, cruel, human nature. I've seen a bit of it in my life—I've never seen it lower than I do now. Drunk? It's a wonder I'm not paralytic!"

"Mr. Gray," I said. "I feel I ought to apologize…"

But Beef would not let me finish.

"There's nothing to apologize for," he said. "They ought to be only too glad I'm not going to ask them questions. There isn't one of them who hasn't got something to hide. There isn't anybody anywhere who hasn't. I would have asked questions, just to tidy up the case. But I'm sick of it now. I've had enough. I'm going to bed instead of asking questions."

Zena Ducrow watching the unhappy Beef, seemed to think that there was entertainment in his condition.

"What sort of questions were you going to ask?" she demanded.

"Never mind now. I'm too tired and too browned off with murder."

I saw the danger of his talking while he was in this condition and said hastily: "If you're tired, Beef, you had better do as you say and take yourself off to bed."

This, of course, made him obstinate, and when Zena repeated, "What sort of questions would they have been?" he looked up muzzily.

"I wanted to know, for instance, which one of you tried to burn a croquet mallet on the night of the twelfth. Not that I don't know already, but I should like to have seen how you answered that."

"But the croquet mallet used to kill Cosmo was found beside him next morning," said Rudolf, staring hard at Beef.

Beef ignored him.

"Then I'd like to have asked about the two people who passed the Gabriels' door together at twenty past twelve that night. I know who they were all right, but I wondered how many of you did. But most of all I wanted to ask how Rudolf's car came to be in a car park at Folkover on the day that Mrs. Ducrow died. Just little things I wanted to know about."

"My car!" shouted Rudolf. "You know that my car had been stolen!"

Beef looked up tipsily.

"I know a lot of things. I was employed to find out who killed Cosmo Ducrow, and I have found out. I was going to tell you all this evening. I'd made arrangements for the big moment when you would hear at last which was the murderer among you. It seemed to be the proper thing to do—all the best detectives believe in it. But I've been told it's something you call 'corny' to do that, so we'll leave it till tomorrow. What about another little drink just to pull me together?"

"He's had quite enough," I said anxiously to Esmeralda.

"You're telling me," she replied.

Gulley gave Beef a weak whisky and water. There was no thought now of letting him go, for intoxicated as he was, he still had the knowledge we all sought.

"You mean," said Gulley, "that although you know the truth you are not going to tell us?"

"Not tonight," said Beef. "Wouldn't do. I'll make my report to Chief Inspector Stute in the morning."

"I would point out," said Theo Gray, "that you are no longer in the police force. Surely your report should first be made to us?"

"Perhaps. But I'm too tired tonight, and it's too complicated. I couldn't get you all to see it. To explain all the details of a murder and a suicide..."

"So Freda wasn't murdered!" broke in Rudolf. "How can you possibly know that?"

Beef looked sheepish.

"I'm talking too much," he said. "And I'm taking up too much of everybody's time. Why, it's twenty to nine!"

At first this sleepy remark did not register with me for Beef did not look in my direction when he made it. Then suddenly with a feeling of guilt I remembered. In ten minutes' time I was due to be in concealment on the roof with the two policemen who were even now waiting in my bedroom. But I realized that since I had never anticipated our still being gathered in one room when the time came, I had no excuse ready.

I stood up and cast about for something to say.

"I wonder if you would mind..." I began. "Perhaps I might ask..."

Beef gave his vulgar guffaw.

"Why don't you say what you want?" he asked. "It's only human, isn't it?"

With flaming cheeks I almost ran from the room.

In spite of this appalling piece of vulgarity I tried to convince myself that Beef was not as drunk as he appeared.

Unless it had been by chance he had effectively reminded me of my appointment and although his last remark to me had been in the worst possible taste it had served, I had to own, to get me out of the room in such a way that no one would suspect an ulterior motive in my departure. Yet his appearance of drunkenness could not be wholly assumed. The truth, I guessed, lay half way between the extremes. He was not drunk enough to forget his arrangements but too drunk to carry them out.

I found Liphook and Constable Spender-Hennessy in my bedroom, their faces rather blank.

"Beef's drunk," I told them.

"Oh, *no!*" said the young constable. "But this is *too* much!"

"I'm afraid so. But he may not be too drunk to carry out his plan, whatever it was. I tried to get something to drink for you fellows, but unfortunately I was caught in the act. Well, we'd better get up on the roof, hadn't we?"

Inspector Liphook seemed to regard the whole thing as childish nonsense and I was more than half inclined to agree with him. Once again I vowed that I would not face the humiliations and difficulties which came from my association with Beef any more after this case was finished. I seemed to have to go from place to place excusing him, trying to defend him, till I looked nearly as foolish as he did. With a wry smile I thought that this evening I had been his apologist first with the suspects and now with the police.

I cautiously opened the door and listened. Down below I could hear a hum of voices from behind the closed door of the room I had left, with Beef's raucous voice audible among them. A baize door cut off the kitchen so I could hear nothing of the Gabriels and Duntons. The rest of the house seemed still and silent. I beckoned to the two men, then led the way along the passage to the staircase leading to the attic floor. In a few minutes the three of us were standing on the bare boards of the upper landing. I pointed to the wooden steps. I felt a certain thrill of excitement as we pulled back the bolts of the upright door at the head of this and crawled out on to the roof. Even if none of the exciting things promised by Beef were to materialize, it was something to be out here in the bright moonlight waiting. Far below us we could see the drive and we knew that the terrace was round the corner of the house. We were not too late in taking up our position for as we settled down I could see that it was just nine minutes to nine. Silence fell.

Beef had given a characteristic answer when Liphook had asked him what we were to expect. "Developments" he had said, no doubt to cover his own uncertainty, and had added "especially on the other wing". I felt that although the event he hoped for would probably take place on the roof, it would be as well to keep an eye on the grounds below us as well and while remaining concealed I looked over the parapet. I could see down into the garage yard and kitchen garden, but although the moonlight made sharp black and silver outlines, it was impossible to distinguish details.

Suddenly I knew that my vigil was rewarded for a streak of yellow light fell across the yard from the back door and someone emerged. I tried hard to identify him and felt pretty certain that I had done so correctly when the man removed all doubt by saying "good night" to those he had left. It was Mills, going across to his own room.

"Hst! Look!" I said to Constable Spender-Hennessy who was beside me.

"Do drop the melodrama," replied this tiresome youth. "Who have you seen? Deadwood Dick?"

"Mills," I whispered.

The chauffeur hesitated, looked about him, then abruptly walked away from his own room to the door leading to the kitchen garden. I lost him in the shadows away to the left.

"Do you think that is what we are waiting to see?" I asked.

"If we have been asked to sit here shivering in order to watch a chauffeur going off for a drink I shall feel that even Beef has excelled himself in bathos."

"How do you know we have not watched a murderer about to commit another crime?"

"I don't know. I'm quite prepared to see Beef stalking the hound of the Baskervilles in a minute, or Sexton Blake jump out of one of those chimneys."

"Not so loud," I cautioned.

Constable Spender-Hennessy dropped his voice to an over-dramatic whisper. "Do you think that Liphook is the murderer?" he asked.

Just then, however, something happened to silence us, something which made me catch my breath and stare across to the roof of the other wing. Very slowly the little door leading to it from the house began to open. Someone was pushing it back so slowly and cautiously that at first it scarcely seemed to move. Then it was right back and we could see the dark shape of a man beginning to climb out.

The two men with me were silent now, breathing rather hard and staring across as fixedly as I was. It was clear that even the constable's flippancy was gone, for in the movements of that slowly moving black shadow was something both fearful and dramatic.

Then from it came an unmistakable rumbling cough and I knew that it was Sergeant Beef.

24

My first thought was that this was some idiotic leg-pull of Beef's, and I was about to stand up and tell him not to be ridiculous when Liphook gripped my arm painfully and whispered, "Shut up! Keep still!" I knew from his voice that he was in earnest.

Now Beef crossed to the parapet and appeared to be rebuttoning his braces. The moon was behind us and lit up his burly outline but it was impossible to see the expression on his face. I felt the tenseness of the moment chiefly through the men beside me for both of them, who had till now made light of the whole affair, were now watching with taut expectation. I did not yet see why this should be, for I had not guessed as they had what would be the next development.

I do not think I was afraid, exactly, but there was a nervous uncontrollable trembling in one of my legs and I was curiously conscious of being very far from the ground. A keen wind was blowing and the low parapet behind which we crouched did not seem to give much protection.

Then, almost as cautiously as Beef had done, someone else began to emerge from the little doorway. We could see nothing but a dark outline slowly increasing in size as the newcomer climbed out on to the roof.

Beef seemed to remain unconscious of this and I was tempted to shout a warning. I might have done so if the two policemen had not seemed so clearly to understand what was going on and to intend that we should in no way reveal our presence. As the newcomer stood up facing Beef, with face still not shown to us, the suspense became intolerable. The parapet was scarcely up to Beefs knees and he appeared to be swaying slightly as though still made unsure by the alcohol he had drunk. While we watched this ugly little scene, in fact, he pulled a bottle out of his pocket and swigged from it.

Then, in a voice which seemed familiar, the newcomer shouted: "You drunken brute!"

Only then did Beef seem fully aware that he was threatened.

"Don't come any closer!" he said, and I could hear the terror in his voice.

He was answered by a contemptuous laugh.

"You don't really think I shall let you leave this roof alive, do you?" said the newcomer. "I can tell you now that your days of detection are finished. You're a blundering ass, but this time you have blundered on a little too much of the truth. In a few minutes there is going to be another suicide. Sergeant Beef is going to throw himself from the roof and no one will ever know that he did not do so of his own accord in a fit of drunken remorse."

"You keep away!" shouted Beef. "It won't do you any good. The police will find out everything, just as I did."

"Not if you are unable to tell them. They haven't yet found out who killed Cosmo Ducrow, have they? And that, after all, is the key to the whole thing. How did you find out, by the way?"

Beef sounded almost hysterical.

"I knew it wasn't you!" he yelled.

"No, it wasn't. But that is the interesting thing. How did you know it wasn't?"

"Never mind now. You keep away from me."

We could see distinctly the newcomer thrust a hand into an overcoat pocket and thereafter hold an arm crooked towards Beef.

"Put that thing away!" Beef shouted wildly. "Put it away, I tell you."

"I hope I shan't have to use it. A shot would not be heard in this wind and you might have shot yourself as easily as thrown yourself over. But it would all be so much more satisfactory and tidy if there was no bullet-hole in you when you were found."

It occurred to me that however much of this scene had been anticipated by Beef, the revolver might be something unforseen.

"Oughtn't we to go across now?" I whispered anxiously to Liphook.

"Not yet," he said grimly.

The newcomer seemed to be in no hurry but stood watching his wretched victim.

"Put that thing away!" Beef shouted again. "Where did you get it from?"

A chuckle came from the dark figure before us.

"Oddly enough, from my own chest-of-drawers. I even have a licence for it. But if I have to use it that won't associate it with me at all. You see, I take precautions. I reported to the police today that it had been stolen. And it will, of course, have your finger-prints on it when it is found beside your corpse."

"Do you mean that you foresaw this?"

"I foresaw that I might have to kill you. I gathered that you knew a little too much. But I never imagined that you would make it as easy as this. A roof-top. So convenient. But I'm glad I've got this little pistol. I would not risk a struggle with you by that parapet. There is a very nasty fall from there to the earth."

"Keep back!" shouted Beef again as the figure moved another step towards him.

"Yes, you've had it now," went on the voice. "You blundered, as I say, on too much truth. But you didn't find one thing which you must have looked for high and low."

"What's that?" asked Beef thickly.

"The suicide note, of course. The little letter written to explain why life was unendurable."

"You kept it?"

"Of course I did. I hoped not to have to produce it, but how could I be sure? It gave too much away but it was there in case some fool found cause to accuse me of murder. I found a safe place for it, though. I don't think you would ever have found it, for I can't imagine you or anyone else in this house reading *The Decline and Fall of the Roman Empire*. However, I don't think it will be necessary now."

"It won't do you any good to kill me," said Beef. "The police will get you—for this too."

"I don't think so. It is unfortunate that you know too much. Ironic, too. You have been floundering on some facts which make your death essential if I am to enjoy peace and leisure."

"You'll never do that!" Beef's voice was high and loud again. "Never. Now stand back!"

The dark figure was very near to him now. It was time, I knew, for us to move. Every instinct of loyalty to my old friend, every scrap of courage, rose in me, and I resolved to risk the levelled pistol and go to Beef's assistance. I opened my mouth to speak but Liphook's hand was over it before I could utter a sound. "Don't move!" he said in a low threatening voice.

I was appalled at his cowardice. How could he watch while Beef was murdered? I knew he had no great opinion of Beef, but to cringe here while my old friend was done to death was contemptible.

"We must!" I tried to say, but the words were muffled.

Then as I watched it happened. The dark figure took a last step forward and by a sudden catlike movement swept Beef's legs from under him and sent him hurtling over the parapet. A sickening cry, like the scream which in nightmares always sticks in one's throat, broke from him as he went back into darkness.

"Oh God!" I cried.

I stood up, not caring now if the pistol was turned on me. I don't know what I shouted to the creature across the parapet, but it must have been loud for at once the figure turned towards me and the moon was full on its evil face. I could not move from where I stood but I saw Liphook and the constable rushing across. I think I was still shouting incoherently and hysterically when I saw that they would be too late, for the murderer had seen them too.

In those few seconds the wretched creature had time to know the game was up. Not only had the murderous attack on Beef been witnessed but words meant only for Beef had been overheard. With a cry like that of a wild beast the murderer sprang towards the parapet. For a few seconds, and just as

Liphook stretched towards the dark outline, it remained in the white glow of moonlight. Then, like a man jumping into water, the thing leapt from the parapet into the darkness of space.

I started to make my way round the chimney stacks to where Liphook and the constable were leaning over the parapet. I scarcely knew why. Beef was dead and it seemed to me suddenly that with him had died a great deal of kindness and decency and sturdy common sense which the sick world could not spare. He had his faults and one of them, his love of beer, had been the cause of his falling a victim to an unscrupulous murderer, quick enough to take advantage of his condition. But with all his faults, his vulgarity, his obstinacy, his childish sense of humour, his rudeness, he remained an honest man, a good detective and a true example of the best in English life and genius. "He was a man, take him for all in all," I said reminiscently, and added: "I shall not look upon his like again."

But there I was wrong. There was something strange in the attitude of Liphook and the constable as they leaned over, something that suggested deep-sea anglers trying to draw in some monstrous fish. And this I found was very much what was happening, for suspended by a steel cable just below the level of our feet was the great weight of Beef, Beef very much alive and quite literally kicking.

I think I must have been a little hysterical from the relief and pleasure of finding my old friend alive for I started to laugh.

"Oh, Beef!" I cried. "You do look funny!"

"You'll look funny when I get up there," spluttered Beef, floundering about like a child trying to swim. "Pull me up for goodness sake, and never mind laughing."

It seemed that the cable was attached to something round his waist for it appeared to come from the small of his back. It took a good deal of manipulation by the three of us and some scrambling by Beef himself to get him at last over the parapet. He at once sat down and blew and gasped from these exertions.

"Good thing the coping juts out a foot or two from the walls of the house," he said at last, "or I could never have done it. It'll take me days to get over the wrenches and bruises as it is."

"So you've come back from the dead," I reflected.

"What's the matter with that?" asked Beef defiantly. "You can't say I don't give you something to write about."

"I don't know. It will be very hard to make this convincing. I shall have to describe you being thrown into space and I don't know how readers will take your resurrection."

"They took it all right from Sherlock Holmes," said Beef. "And he hadn't got a steel cable like I have."

Liphook smiled.

"Did you expect the suicide?" he asked.

"No. Can't say I did," Beef was honest enough to admit. "Still it may be just as well. I doubt if we would have got a conviction for murder. Now help me out of this thing."

Beef stood up and took off his jacket which was ripped at the back. We saw an elaborate arrangement round his trunk, a sort of canvas strait waistcoat which went from his armpits to his thighs.

"My idea," he said proudly, "though young Bomb helped me fix it. Couldn't have done it without. Anything narrow would have cut me in two. Well, let's go down and pick up the pieces."

25

B eef now began to behave like a hero returning in triumph. He led the way downstairs, and before even going to examine the body lying on the terrace he announced that he needed a drink.

"First today?" I asked mischievously.

"Not so far from it," he replied with good-humour, "though I had to have enough to make me look as though I'd had too much. I'm not so good an actor that I could have come in and convinced even you, Townsend, that I was drunk if I hadn't been a little bit. See, I know just how much I can take. Not like some people. What I needed was the right amount to make me look a bit lit, but not so much that I couldn't do my part. Yes, I'll have a nice drop of Scotch for a change. Well, here's to all the suspects who aren't guilty."

I noticed that Inspector Liphook seemed to treat Beef with a new respect, while even Constable Spender-Hennessy made no more sarcastic remarks. We waited until Beef had finished his drink then allowed ourselves to be led through the french windows on to the stone-flagged terrace.

Here a very loathsome sight awaited us. The suicide had fallen on his back and lay now with blood around his head and eyes staring glassily up to the night sky. It was the man whose voice I had heard speaking to Beef on the roof. It was Theo Gray.

I make no apology for my first reaction to this sight. I felt no pity for the dead man and only a queasy horror at the gruesome appearance of his corpse. I turned at once to Beef and said: "But this means you've cheated. You specifically stated that Theo Gray did not kill Cosmo Ducrow."

"No more he didn't," said Beef.

"Then I give up," I said. "It's too difficult."

Beef grinned and without touching the corpse, which Liphook had examined, led the way back into the house.

"I asked them all to stay in the dining-room," said Beef. "It would never have done to have them hopping about while I was arranging things. You can let 'em out now," he added grandly.

Liphook went off to telephone to Stute and to arrange for Gray's corpse to be removed, while I went to the dining-room and said as politely as possible that Sergeant Beef would be glad if they would care to come through to the library as he had some news for them.

"Another murder?" asked Gulley.

"Very nearly," I replied. "Fortunately only a suicide this time, though."

"Where is Theo?" demanded Rudolf Ducrow.

I was not sure whether Beef wished me to give any details of events so I said simply: "He's gone out, I think," which, in a way, was true.

When we filed into the library Beef rose from his chair and said to Rudolf: "I should like the staff to come in for this."

"For what?"

"For what I'm going to tell you."

"And what is that?" asked Rudolf with a suggestion of scorn in his voice.

Beef looked rather menacing.

"I'm going to tell you who killed Cosmo Ducrow."

"At last," said Rudolf. "Very well, we'll gather them all here."

When the Duntons and Gabriels came in it was obvious that their reconciliation was no pretence for the two women sat down side by side. The men also appeared to be on the best of terms. Mills sat on a hard chair away from the rest of them.

"I must apologize for being a bit umpty earlier in the evening," said Beef. "It was necessary to make someone believe I was drunk, and so that I shouldn't have to take any chances, I *got* drunk. I mean, that's the way to be convincing, isn't it? You will nearly all be glad to hear that this piece of acting was highly successful and that a murderous attack was made on me not half an hour ago.

"Well, now, about this case. Most of you are longing to know the whole truth, just as I was when I started on it. And very soon I realized that I was up against something particularly difficult and someone fiendishly clever. I was pretty sure that nothing had been planned before the night of the twelfth because on that night something led to Cosmo Ducrow's death which could not have been anticipated unless there was a fairly wide conspiracy amongst you. That something was his learning of his wife's infidelity with his nephew."

Ernest Wickham broke in.

"Is there any need to refer to intimate matters of that kind? *De mortuis*, you know."

"We can't mince matters now, Mr. Wickham. As I was saying, I did not think that Cosmo's death had been planned, yet there was a perfection about the scheme which I could scarcely believe had come from what you might call improvising. This perfection continued to be evident throughout the whole case. Even after the death of Mrs. Ducrow I knew that the question I had to answer, the key to the whole puzzle, remained the same. *Who killed Cosmo Ducrow?"*

Just then a prolonged ringing of the front-door bell interrupted him. He guessed, I suppose, that it was someone who had come in response to Liphook's phone calls, and decided to break the news of Gray's death to all his listeners. This he did in a characteristically crude manner.

"Oh, by the way," he said. "Theo Gray's dead."

Since he had not first explained that Gray was guilty this was a most shocking way to make his announcement.

Rudolf jumped to his feet.

"Murdered?" he said in a loud rising voice.

Beef did not turn a hair.

"No. Suicide," he said.

Gulley was excited now.

"That I will not believe. You may be able to convince me that Mrs. Ducrow took her own life, but not Theo. He was far too... too sane. Too cool a man."

"He was cool all right," said Beef, "and as you'll see later he was guilty."

"You mean, you're going to try and make us believe that Theo murdered Cosmo Ducrow?"

"No. I'm not going to try to make you believe anything."

"Then what was he guilty of?"

"Murdering me," said Beef calmly.

"For God's sake stop this clowning!"

"No clowning about it. He pushed me off the roof with three witnesses. I mean, witnessed by three people."

Gulley spoke as though he were clinching an argument with a lunatic.

"Then would you kindly explain how you come to be standing here, alive and well?"

It would be impossible to describe all the peasant cunning, the grinning mysteriousness, the sheer boyish artfulness that Beef managed to show in his face and voice as he made his triumphant reply.

"Ah!" he said.

Gabriel meanwhile had been out to open the front door. He returned now with Stute and two stretcher bearers. The gathering broke up into smaller conferences and on all sides I heard expressions of incredulity about Gray's guilt.

"It makes you think, though, doesn't it?" said Mrs. Gabriel, "I mean that's three gone. You wonder who the next will be. It's all very well to talk about suicide, but it's a bit of a coincidence, isn't it?"

"You're right," replied Mrs. Dunton. "It's more like a madman at work. If what he says is true and Mr. Gray pushed him off the roof he wouldn't be alive now to tell the tale, so what's the good of talking? It's more likely *he* murdered Mr. Gray, if you ask me."

"And such a nice gentleman," said Mrs. Gabriel. "In all the years he's lived here and I've been here we've never had a bit of trouble. He was a real gentleman, I will say that. Not like some."

"No. That's a fact."

I left them nodding at one another with tight lips and meaning eyes.

The stretcher party had done its work, taking the remains of Theo Gray out by the back way. But Stute remained. He sounded annoyed with Beef.

"If you had told me what you were up to I certainly shouldn't have agreed to the Inspector coming here. We can't have Special Branch men watching suicide."

"It was murder I wanted them to watch," argued Beef. "And they watched it. I had my reasons, Inspector, as you'll hear if you like to stay on a little while. I'm just going over the case to them all."

"Oh, you are? You've got it all taped?"

"I think so."

"You know who killed Cosmo Ducrow?"

"Yes. I know that."

"You are going to name him or her?"

"Yes."

"Then I'll stay. I like to have my job done for me. Do you think there will be any more violence tonight?"

"No. I don't think so."

"We don't want another suicide."

"There won't be any more."

"Very well. You can go ahead with your exposition."

"Will you all take your seats again, please? The cadaver has been removed. I am about to clear up the whole of this mystery for you."

A silence fell on the room. I looked round once more at those tense and anxious faces, wondering which member of Beef's audience would be named. Gray was "guilty", Beef said. But of what? Not of murdering Cosmo. Perhaps he had killed Freda Ducrow? Yet Beef himself had spoken of one murder and one suicide and of the suicide note which Gray said had been left. Did his guilt lie only in his actions after someone else had committed the greater crime of murder? Had he but taken advantage of the violence of others? If so, there was a murderer yet to be named, and again I found myself looking round the room in desperation, trying to pick out the guilty one before Beef did so. Gulley? He looked distraught and guilty enough. Rudolf? I did not want to believe it of him for I had always admired and liked his frank open disposition. Mills? I had to admit that he was my choice, if any. Gabriel? A dark horse this, and he had had every opportunity. Dunton? The big heavy fellow looked like a killer to me. Ernest Wickham? Why not? He could have been here that night for all we knew, and it was curious that Beef had insisted on his presence this evening. Or was it one of the women? The big muscular Zena? The fierce-looking Mrs. Dunton? Little bitter Mrs. Gabriel? Attractive Esmeralda Tobyn? It could be anyone, I supposed.

But Beef knew. However foolish he might have been, he knew now and would tell us the truth. I, no less than the others, was agog to hear his story.

"Yes," he said. "I have never doubted that the key to this whole mystery lay in the answer to that question—who killed Cosmo Ducrow? Even now when we have had this violence tonight and I have been thrown over the parapet of the roof I know that the riddle could never be solved unless I can answer that. And I can. The funny thing is that I got it first as you're trying to get it now—by guesswork. A little thing made me think, and I saw the whole secret. It was guesswork which suggested it, but I'm going to produce a lot more than guesswork to prove it to you all tonight.

"Still, I'll start off with what I guessed. Very early in the case I guessed that the answer to the question which we were all asking ourselves, the answer to the question, Who Killed Cosmo Ducrow? was... Cosmo Ducrow."

26

B eef, of course, expected this to gain an effect, and he was not disappointed. To describe the faces around him I can only use the old-fashioned adjective "spellbound". Rudolf was the first to pull himself together.

"Look here," he said. "I don't know if you're trying to be funny. But if you think that a man can bash in the back of his own skull with a croquet mallet you must be out of your mind. Surely if ever a murder was obvious it was this one?"

"That's the point. It was obvious. A little too obvious. Murderers don't as a rule leave their weapons for everyone to see. Nor do they use about six times the violence that is necessary. That was what made me think. I soon realized what made this case unique. *Most murderers try to make murder look like suicide. Someone here had tried to make suicide look like murder.*"

"Very neat," said Stute. "But have you any proof of this?"

"Until tonight I hadn't much. Just bits of circumstantial evidence. But now, luckily, I think I can give you all the proof we shall need. That is if Mr. Townsend will just hand me a book called *The Declining Empire*, or something of the sort."

"You mean Gibbon's *Decline and Fall*. Which volume do you want?"

"Eh?" said Beef nervously.

"It's in ten volumes."

"Let's have the lot, then."

It was not long before he had flicked over the pages and pulled out a loose sheet of paper from one of the volumes. When he had read this he handed it to Stute. Later I was able to copy it:

"It is one o'clock. Not much more than an hour ago I was a fairly happy man. I now know that I was a most deluded one and that my wife has been deceiving me for a long time, and that the nephew whom I trusted is a blackguard. I have discussed this with only one man, and he alone knows that I mean to die by my own hand and at once, tonight. It is the best way out. I want no further part in a life which can do this to me."

"Cosmo Ducrow."

"Is that proof enough?"

"So long as this is the man's handwriting."

"Thanks," said Beef. "So you see my first guess was right. Now I'd better go back to the beginning of the case and tell you what happened.

"That night was, as Gray said, like any other night up to the time when Gray left Cosmo in the library with his stamps. This was a fairly happy household, for Cosmo Ducrow knew nothing of his nephew's behaviour, and Gray, though he had made a careful study of crime and murder methods, was not a man to show his hand. He was content if necessary to wait for his friend's death to inherit his share of a great fortune.

I say 'if necessary', for I think that he had worked out a few little schemes which he might be able to put into effect in certain circumstances.

"Now on this particular night Zena Ducrow decided to go and tackle Cosmo about her husband. In fairness to her I must say that I believe her entirely when she says she never dreamed that Cosmo did not know. Everyone else did, including the staff. It seemed impossible that Cosmo should not. So without saying anything to her husband Zena walked across the park with one of her dogs. Freda Ducrow, up in her bedroom which overlooks the terrace, heard her whistling the animal in the unmistakable way she has. Naturally enough, instead of waking the servants she went to the french windows of the library, tapped, and was admitted by Cosmo. She has told us quite frankly of the conversation which followed and of Cosmo's shock on hearing about his wife. Then she went back by a roundabout way, not wishing to meet her husband. She knew he would be coming up to the house at this time.

"Cosmo knew that, too, and knew from Zena probably that he was admitted through the back door by the Gabriels. Cosmo waited, saw Rudolf cross the kitchen and go up the back stairs. That was enough confirmation of Zena's story. He was sure now that the worst was true.

"Now before we go any farther, I was wondering if we couldn't have a nice cup of tea? It's dry work this, and a cup of tea would go down a treat. What do you say, Mr. Ducrow?" He turned to Rudolf as, presumably, the house's new owner. "After all, I was employed to clear you of the murder of Cosmo Ducrow and I've done so. Am I asking too much?"

Rudolf managed to answer with a faint and not very friendly smile. "What about it, Mrs. Gabriel?"

"I'm sure we could all do with a cup, Mr. Rudolf. I'll nip and put the kettle on."

"I'll slip out and help you," said Mrs. Dunton.

Cigarettes were lit and a buzz of conversation started while we waited. There was no more incredulity now, only impatience to hear the rest.

"For a murdered man you're bearing up very well," I said to Beef.

"I wish I felt it. I'm a mass of bruises, and I've got a cold coming on. But we'll get this over."

The women returned with a large tray, and Beef was soon lapping at a breakfast cup full of black sweet tea.

"Cosmo was a man to trust his friends, and feeling himself betrayed by his nephew he decided to consult his lifelong crony Theo Gray. But in order to get to his room by the usual way he would have to pass his wife's door, so he decided to use the back staircase. He crept up, called Theo out and the two went downstairs together. That was why Mrs. Gabriel heard *one* set of footsteps going up and *two* coming down again.

"I am not even going to guess what took place between them, except to say that I don't think Gray tried very hard to dissuade his old friend from suicide. I think, in fact, that when Gray left him later he knew not only that Cosmo was going to kill himself but also where and how.

"That, I must admit at once, is more than I know. We shall, I suppose, soon be able to establish by a post mortem how it was done, though Gray covered this up pretty well. When a doctor sees a man with no back of the cranium at all but a mass of splintered bone and brain he is not likely to look for any other cause of death. It may be that Cosmo poisoned himself, for there were sleeping tablets in the house, or it may even be that he shot himself with Gray's pistol, conveniently lent for the occasion. If he had put the barrel between his lips and fired through the roof of his mouth it is possible that the battering of his head would conceal all signs of it.

"As to where this happened, I would not like to guess. If it was a shot it must have been down by the little pavilion, I think, or someone would have heard it. If it was poison it could have been in the house, for Gray could have carried that thin little body down to the pavilion after death. At all events, Cosmo did as one might expect a man of his neurotic and mis—misan——"

"Misanthropic," I whispered quickly.

"And misanthropic nature to do—he committed suicide, and Theo Gray knew that he had. He was clever enough to see in that his chance."

There was another pause while Beef refilled his cup.

"Mr. Townsend's a writer," he went on presently, "and I daresay he could give you a picture of the criminal's mind. He could very likely explain with bags of psychology just what made Gray do what he did. To me it's still a bit of a puzzle. He was going to get a third of Cosmo's fortune anyway, and that would make him a rich man. Why risk anything for more? A part of the answer is that he wasn't risking anything. He could put the little letter which Cosmo had left on his table safely tucked away in a book which no one was likely to take down, so that if ever he were accused of Cosmo's murder he could clear himself. What he planned to do, therefore, entailed no risk to him, even if it was discovered that he had had something to do with it.

"What he saw was this. If Cosmo's suicide could be made to look like murder only one man would be suspected, and that was Rudolf Ducrow. Get him hanged for it, and there would be another third share in the kitty. And with Rudolf in the house now and going home across the park later it would be the easiest thing in the world to pin it on Rudolf.

"Cosmo's body was down by the pavilion. Whether he had killed himself there or whether Gray moved the corpse does not much matter at this point. Gray thought out his plan carefully and went to work. He remembered seeing an old jacket of Rudolf's which had been hanging in the cloak-room since last summer. This, he thought, would be a first means of associating Rudolf with the crime. He put it on under his overcoat and went out through the french windows. No one saw him at this time, but if anyone had seen him I feel sure they would have noticed that he carried an open umbrella. This effectively concealed his identity from any possible observer above him.

"He made his way to the pavilion and decided that the corpse should appear to have been battered to death with a croquet mallet. He was wearing gloves, but realized that if he used Rudolf's mallet he would smudge the fingerprints from it, so he picked up another mallet, one of no particular significance, and used it to smash in the dead man's skull. When I came later to try the game of croquet I decided that the blows dealt to Cosmo's head were only likely to have been given if the head was on the ground in the position of a croquet ball. Having done that he took Rudolf's mallet, blooded it, and holding it gingerly all the time, left it by the corpse. Then he also stained the sleeve of the jacket with Cosmo's blood and left the dead man there.

"Gray forgot nothing. He took the mallet which he had actually used for smashing in Cosmo's skull and carried it back to the house. As he approached and knew that he might be in view of the windows, he put up his umbrella and made his way to the garage yard. He broke the handle of the mallet and pushed it with the round smooth hammer part into the furnace, feeling certain that they would be completely destroyed in a few minutes. We owe our knowledge of this part of his action to Mills, whose curiosity took him down to see what had been burnt. Unfortunately he could not recover the mallet from the flames. It would have made a nice exhibit.

"Gray returned to his room unheard by Freda and Rudolf, locked the jacket away somewhere, and sat down to await Rudolf's departure.

"The next part of his plan was daring and clever. He had to make sure that Rudolf was seen going home across the park. It occurred to him that there might otherwise be no evidence of Rudolf's presence in the house that night, for Freda Ducrow was scarcely likely to reveal it, and the Gabriels might not be able to say for certain that he had come. So he waited, listening for Rudolf to leave Freda Ducrow's room, then, when he knew that Rudolf was clear of the house, he hurried down and telephoned Dunton with a story about shouts in the park. Dunton was to keep a look-out, which meant that he would just about be in time to see Rudolf returning to his house.

"Gray had a piece of luck here, for Mrs. Dunton had returned to the lodge that night and she and her husband had a great deal to talk over. They were still up when Gray telephoned, so that Dunton was in plenty of time to see Rudolf. Rudolf looked a bit put out and nervous, but that was natural enough in the circumstances. So Gray was able to go to bed that night feeling very pleased with himself. The event he had been awaiting for years, the death of Cosmo, had come to pass with no assistance from him, and by a few little touches here and there he had pinned it on one of the three inheritors of Cosmo's money whose share, in the event

of his death, would swell the incomes of himself and Freda
Ducrow. He had the suicide note in case, as a last resort, he
needed it. He must have slept well that night.

"On his way back to his room after telephoning Dunton
he met Freda Ducrow, who had heard him go downstairs and
thought he was following Rudolf. She was relieved to hear
that it was only some shouting he had heard and that he had
telephoned Dunton about it. He did not mind her seeing him
because in any case he was going to be quite open about his
call to Dunton.

"No, there was nothing to disturb his sleep. Not even the
fact that he had perhaps helped his oldest friend to kill himself
and had planned to get an innocent man hanged for his death.
I told you tonight that there are times when I want to forget
this thing called human nature. Gray has made one of those
times for me. I hope you're getting all this down, Townsend?
Don't miss that bit about human nature, will you? I meant
what I said about that."

27

"We come now," said Beef pompously, "to the small part played in this affair by Major Gulley."

Rather tactlessly everyone turned to stare at Gulley, who looked like an embarrassed walrus.

"He came motoring down from London with his friend Miss Tobyn exactly as he had described, quite unconscious that anything was amiss at Hokestones. I don't think that on his side this night trip was quite as impulsive as he has maintained, because the cottage must have been prepared to receive her."

"As a matter of fact it was quite on impulse," interrupted Gulley in his plummy voice. "The cottage was more or less ready, but we had had no idea of using it that night."

"It doesn't matter," said Beef. "The point is that at five o'clock in the morning Gulley was coming up the drive with his headlights on when he turned a bend and his lights showed him someone lying on the grass near the pavilion. He pulled up, went across and found that it was the remains of Cosmo Ducrow, with blood clotted and cold round the head. It was an unpleasant sight for anyone to come on in the small hours, and Gulley quite lost his head. He knew that certain matters connected with his running of the estate were being examined, and he saw himself accused of murdering Cosmo because of them. He was foolish enough to drive straight back to London in the hope that his visit to Hawden during the night would never be known. Fortunately Miss Tobyn had more sense than he had, and made a clean breast of it. That is all that either of them had to do with the death of Cosmo Ducrow. But you may have noticed what a nasty turn it gave Gray when I first mentioned that car. It was something he did *not* know about, and it might produce all sorts of complications.

"But to return to the days following the death of Cosmo Ducrow. At first it seemed to Gray that everything was going according to plan. It was clear that the police suspected Rudolf and that an arrest might be expected at any minute. But when that arrest did not come he grew anxious. It was then he decided that the jacket must be found, and he called me in to find it.

"I never like a case where I'm expected to clear someone, and I distrusted Gray's motives from the first. I soon began to think that so far from wanting to avoid Rudolf's arrest he was impatient for it. I did not like the way he spoke well of everyone. No one could have been a murderer, he implied, Gulley, Gabriel, everybody was too good to be true. I wondered at first whether he could have murdered Cosmo and then made it look as though Rudolf had done it. But no, Gray was too confident, too smug to have committed murder then. And why not? For as we know now, all the time he had that suicide note to fall back on if the worst came to the worst.

"On my first morning here he decided to fetch Rudolf Ducrow 'in case I should be ready to see him that morning', though I hadn't said anything about seeing him then. That afternoon when I went down to Rudolf's lodge I found the old jacket in the cloakroom. Gray had asked me to take Rudolf's gun away from him, and I believed I understood the reason—it was because the gun was in the cloakroom, and in getting it I should see the jacket. Gray had studied my methods. He knew that I shouldn't miss a light-coloured jacket hanging among overcoats. He may even have guessed that I should have found out about it having hung up at Hokestones."

There was a sudden "Oo!" from Mrs. Gabriel.

"I've just thought of something. I mentioned to Mr. Gray about that jacket having gone, and he said be sure and tell you about it! Why didn't I think of that before?"

"Why didn't you?" echoed Beef sternly. "Well, that accounts for it. Gray roughly cleaned it, and on going down to Rudolf's that morning left it in the cloakroom for me to find. He knew I'd report it to Stute and thought now the case against Rudolf would be cast iron. Well, it was. But just a little too cast-iron. As usual, he had overdone it. The case was so damning that Chief Inspector Stute suspected a plant. So the arrest of Rudolf was still delayed while further investigations were made.

"I was interested to notice that as soon as I had found the jacket Gray wanted me to give up the case, and offered me liberal terms to do so. I had been useful—now I might learn too much. I decided to stick to it, and from that time onward I was very much on my guard."

Ernest Wickham was the next to interrupt.

"This is all very interesting," he said, "but I am chiefly concerned with the death of Freda Ducrow. It is growing late, and so far all we have learnt is that Cosmo Ducrow committed suicide and that Theo Gray tried to make it look like murder in order to implicate Rudolf. Perhaps you are going to suggest that in Mrs. Ducrow's case it was the same."

"No. Vice verse."

"You mean?"

It was natural for the solicitor to ask, for Beef had sounded as though he were speaking of immoral poetry.

"I mean that Cosmo's death was suicide made to look like murder. Freda Ducrow's was murder made to look like suicide."

"I see. Perhaps you had better continue in your own way."

"Perhaps I had. I wish my little chat with Gray on the roof tonight had been longer because there was so much I wanted to know which only he could tell me. For instance, at what point it occurred to him that he need not stop at getting *half* Cosmo's fortune but could now get the whole lot. I imagine that it may have been at the very moment when Freda Ducrow announced that if anything happened to Rudolf she would commit suicide. That may have given him the idea. Why shouldn't she? It would leave him still unsuspected and with a clear field.

"His first preparation for this was to get hold of Rudolf's car. Even if Rudolf had been arrested before he needed to use it it would be better than using his own. For he knew that in order to arrange Freda's death he would have to be in some place other than where he was supposed to be. So he went out that night, using his open umbrella trick in case he was recognized from the house. Townsend saw him but hadn't the sense to wake me. If he had I would have known who was absent and the case would have been broken open far sooner than it was.

"Then having taken the car he drove it to London, put it into one of the large all-night garages where it would attract no attention at all, and came down by the first train. He was an early bird, this Gray. You remember on the morning after Mrs. Ducrow's disappearance he walked in as we were finishing breakfast. On this morning he was too clever to do that. He stopped at the pavilion, left his hat and coat there, then appeared on the terrace with his usual newspaper as though he had gone out for a minute's air before breakfast. (His umbrella he had left in the car, I think.) Townsend, in fact, met him on the terrace but was too busy trying to find footprints to take much notice of him. Nor was Townsend much interested when I found the coat and hat in the pavilion and saw they had disappeared by the following evening.

"Gray intended to wait until Rudolf was arrested before arranging the 'suicide' of Freda Ducrow, because that would make it all the more natural. Besides he imagined that he only had to wait until the expert's report on the jacket came through. But before any arrest he was given an opportunity which was too good to miss. Freda decided to go down to Folkover to see Mr. Wickham and asked Gray to phone for an appointment. He knew that she would be leaving Wickham's office some time after five-thirty.

"Then he had what he thought was another piece of luck— we were going to London that day ourselves and would see him go there. And this is where I have to confess to a piece of blindness which may have cost a human life. For some reason it never occurred to me that he was going down to Folkover. I was pretty sure of my man by this time. I even saw Freda Ducrow's danger and begged her not to talk of suicide. But I never dreamed that Gray would strike before Rudolf's arrest, and I never thought of him going up to London then down to Folkover. Mr. Townsend could explain that psychologically.

Something to do with their being in opposite directions. But there you are, I've got to own I missed it.

"What Gray did, of course, was to leave us at the station, have lunch at his club or at some place where they would remember him, then get out Rudolf's car and make for Folkover. He parked round the corner, as I knew later from the infant prodigy whose hobby was car-spotting, then waited for Freda to leave Mr. Wickham's office.

"He did not know she was meeting Gulley at six, but when she told him he could soon talk her out of that. He had been so worried about her, he said, that he had come down to find her and talk things over.

"His next two hours were the most difficult. He had to wait until about nine to be sure of Greynose Point being deserted, but he daren't go to any bar with her for fear of being recognized afterwards. There was only one answer with Freda Ducrow and he had prepared for it. A bottle of whisky in the car. He had only to suggest that they should drive up on the downs and drink it and the thing was easy. By nine o'clock Freda Ducrow was hopelessly drunk in her own car on the grass near Greynose Point and so far as anyone could know, Theo Gray was in London.

"It's not pleasant to think of the next part. I imagine he took no chances. First he made sure that no one was in sight—and in any case he had turned the car lights off hours earlier. Then I think he probably rendered Freda Ducrow unconscious, for no blow on the head that he gave her now would be distinguishable after that fearful fall through space. Then all he had to do was start the car, put off the handbrake and shove it over. There was a slight downward slope towards the cliff edge at the spot he chose which would have made it easy.

"There was a risk of the car bursting into flames and attracting attention at once. But even then, he calculated, an elderly gentleman with an umbrella taking an evening stroll would attract no notice. And in any case, it didn't catch fire.

"Now his course was clear—but as usual he slightly overdid the taking of precautions, and his open umbrella as he passed the Greynose Point Hotel was remembered by George. But he had an easy drive back to London in time to be at the flat, as it happened, when we phoned through at midnight to tell him that Freda Ducrow was missing. I still had no idea that he had had anything to do with it, and not until Rudolf's car was found at Cinderhurst Station, where he had left it before getting on a Hawden train that morning, did I see how he could have been there.

"Of course, he was clever enough to join with the rest of you in saying that it could not be suicide, knowing that his opinion would not make any difference one way or the other when the police came to decide. That was his policy, just as it had been his policy to say that Rudolf would not have killed Cosmo. Subtle, that's what he was."

28

" I saw it all," said Beef, "but there was not a chance of getting a conviction. Even if I could prove that Cosmo had committed suicide and that Gray had made it look like murder it would not help much. I might have been able to prove that much, because the person who burnt the mallet could have been no one else. Everyone had an alibi for that time—except Zena Ducrow, perhaps. But it would not have given me much satisfaction to get him on a minor charge. As for the murder of Freda—I hadn't a hope of proving it. I might produce evidence that Gray had left Rudolf's car in London and taken it out that day. I might even show that he had been in Folkover with it. But there would be no way of making a jury believe beyond doubt that he had deliberately stunned Freda and pushed her car over Greynose Point. My own evidence for that was highly circumstantial.

"But I was not going to let him get away with it altogether, and I worked out this little scheme by which he would at least do a few years in prison for attempted murder, even if we should achieve no more.

"I had to take someone into my confidence, so I went to Bomb Mills and between us we fixed up the little gadget which three of you saw used. We made a sort of rough waistcoat of sailcloth coming to a loop behind, then looped a steel cable round the chimney stack. The cable had a spring hank on it so that all I had to do when I was ready was to attach the hook to the loop in the small of my back and there we were.

"Then I had to show Gray that I had got him taped. I got a little bit tiddly, pretended to be a good deal more, and brought out in my conversation that I knew about the burnt croquet mallet, about him and Cosmo going downstairs that night and about Rudolf's car in the car-park at Folkover. Also I made it clear that I had not yet reported these things to the police. That was quite enough. He saw, as I wanted him to do, that his only chance of avoiding arrest was to kill me this evening.

"You may think I was underrating the intelligence of a man who had shown himself a very clever murderer. I don't think so. You see, with a man like that I can be sure of one thing—he will underrate me. Mr. Townsend always writes up my cases as though I was a half-wit who luckily tumbles on the solution, and though Gray did not think quite that, he didn't suppose I was much of a match for him. And, as I say, I was a little drunk—he saw I wasn't acting the part.

"With everything ready on the roof and witnesses hidden on the roof of the other wing, I did my stuff downstairs then furtively crept away..."

Beef's expression as he said this resembled that of the demon barber of Fleet Street, and there was a little laughter in the room. He took that in good humour.

"Well, I did," he said. "Bit staggery on my feet, but furtive as a fox at the same time. That got him, and he followed me upstairs as I hoped he would. When he saw me going out on the roof he must have been tickled to death and thought his luck was in again. I was a few minutes ahead of him, though, and had time to attach the spring hank to the loop before he appeared."

"I thought you were buttoning your braces!" I said.

Beef spoke with lofty reproof.

"There's no need to be vulgar," he said.

Coming from him this was doubly hard to bear, but before I could protest he continued.

"So there I was, ready for him. I had been practising this falling trick with Bomb in the morning, first in the garage and then up here on the roof. I'd got to the point where I could go over the edge without risk, though I'd taken some hard knocks at first. It is not as difficult as it looks. You might try it if you want to be murdered some time.

"One precaution we had taken while you were all in at dinner; we had gone and fired off all the rounds in Gray's revolver. I had one nasty turn this evening when I thought at first the pistol he brought out was another one. I was pretty relieved when he said where he had got it.

"I had warned the Detective Inspector and the constable, of course, but not Mr. Townsend, because he describes things so much better when they come as a surprise to him, as they nearly always do. I'd had to tell Inspector Liphook to keep him quiet at all costs, though, and once he nearly had to sock him to do it. But as you have all noticed, Mr. Townsend is a gentleman with a keen sense of humour and was not offended."

What could I do, after this heavy-handed compliment, but take it all in good part? I smiled and nodded, and Beef continued.

"Well, it all worked out a treat. Gray came for me as I stood in front of the parapet and, as far as he ever knew, murdered me. Then, when he saw Inspector Liphook and the constable, he gave us all a surprise and threw himself from the roof. This was unexpected, for as Major Gulley said just now he was too sane and cool a man for suicide.

"That completes the case, ladies and gentlemen, and I for one am not sorry. I've known a good many murderers, but this one gave me the willies. He was the patient kind, prepared to wait for years to get what he wanted. All the time he lived with you you never saw him as anything but a quiet, pleasant gentleman who would not hurt a fly. I don't suppose he would unless it got in his way. But the moment he saw his chance—then it was a different matter. His timing was nothing less than brilliant. He could not have chosen a better moment for ridding himself of Freda Ducrow, and he nearly brought off the whole scheme."

Stute was the first to congratulate Beef, but pointed out that as a free-lance investigator he had been able to use methods denied to the police, also that he had followed what was no more than a hunch in the first place, a thing that was usually to be deplored. Wickham added his congratulations, but with another reservation.

"If we had known your conclusions about Gray," he pointed out, "we might have saved Freda Ducrow."

I felt that I should reply to this.

"Surely you are opening up a big question, are you not? And the Sergeant must be exhausted. After all he has practised his fall, got himself partially intoxicated, been thrown from a rooftop and given a long and lucid explanation of the case all in the space of twelve hours. I think he deserves a rest."

This clinched the matter, and the strange gathering began to break up. For the first time since I had come to Hokestones I slept with an unlocked door and a sense of relief that the evil in the house had gone for ever.

There is little more to relate about the Ducrow Case. The Press and the crime-reading public had a Roman holiday with the sensational events of that night, which was some consolation to them, perhaps, for the loss of an intricate trial for murder. Rudolf, now a very rich man, showed himself a generous one in respect of Beef's fees, for when his cheque came he had doubled our charges. He and Zena have moved into Hokestones which, I am told, is now full of dogs. The Gabriels have remained with them and Mrs. Dunton has returned to her duties in the house.

There is another aspect of this remarkably happy ending which I record with pleasure. Gulley and his attractive girl friend are to be married as soon as their respective divorces come through. Esmeralda has realized her dream, for the cottage she was to have seen on that night of the 12th is now surrounded with acres of flowers which she grows for "Esmé's", her little shop in Church Road.

So Beef is back in Lilac Road waiting, he says, for the next case. "I hope I shan't have to be murdered again," he says devoutly. His wife seems less decided on this point, for she has never approved of his work as a private detective and hankers after a little general shop somewhere so that he would not be called out to investigate these nasty messy murders.

"Will's always been the same," she says to me. "Playacting half the time and thinking he's a real detective. I tell him he'll get into trouble one of these days. Murder's a funny thing, isn't it?"

I know what she means, so I look quite serious as I reply: "Very funny. Very funny indeed."

Beef only winks.